Sister Mid

♦

Jeremy Reed

velvet

SISTER MIDNIGHT
Jeremy Reed
ISBN 1 871592 80 1
Copyright © Jeremy Reed 1997
First edition 1998
Copyright © Velvet Publicationss 1998
All rights reserved
Published by
VELVET PUBLICATIONS
83 Clerkenwell Road
London EC1, UK
Tel: 0171-430-9878
Fax: 0171-242-5527
♦

Design: Bradley Davis, PCP International
A Bondagebest Production

CONTENTS

Part I
DEEP NIGHT
5

Part II
TORCHSONG EXTRAVAGANZA
27

Part III
THE UNDERWORLD
47

Part IV
THE HAREM
69

Part V
CYBERLIBRARY
89

Part VI
NEW DAY
109

Appendix
MORE TALES OF THE MIDGET
127

Alice Through The Looking Glass
129

Catching Stars
137

After Wilde's Trial
147

> "A voice is like a dress;
> playing a record is sonic drag."
> —Wayne Koestenbaum

> "If you want to buy my wares
> Follow me and climb the stairs
> Love for sale"
> —Cole Porter

> "My life a wreck you're making,
> you know I'm yours for the taking:
> I'd gladly surrender myself for you,
> body and soul."
> —*Body And Soul*

Part I

DEEP NIGHT

Autumn. A thwack of red leaves flapped like stranded fish on the cracked architrave.

Marciana stood in front of a full length heart-shaped mirror, decorated with gilt angels, and with both hands in the small of her back, reached for the taut zip on her skirt. In a lightning-flurry of red sequins the garment dropped at her feet. She disengaged her four inch heels from the pooled skirt, as though she was stepping out of a flower, and admiringly reviewed herself back and front in the mirror.

'I'm Sade's sister,' Marciana kept repeating to herself. She ran a finger up each black seam to where the stocking top was held tight by a six drop suspender belt. She liked the rigidity of the three plated metal clips on each thigh. The black funeral urn tattooed on her left buttock showed through the window of her transparent panties.

When Marciana took off her stockings she liked to imagine that the tongues of big cats were licking her thighs. Lions, leopards, panthers and jaguars. She bunched her stockings into two silk cocoons, unfastened the hook and eye of her suspender belt, and all the time watching her actions in the mirror, unclipped her bra, and let the two roses of her nipples tumble into arrested contact with the air.

She flopped back on the bed with her legs wide open. Julie London's sultry phrasing was addressing the standard

'Black Coffee' on the CD release of *After Midnight*. This subdued diva's perfect diction entered Marciana so deeply that at times she imagined that she herself was responsible for the song, and not the woman in tight black slacks depicted on the cover, who had recorded the number circa 1960.

Julie would float with consummate ease into 'Don't Smoke In Bed' and 'After Midnight' with a coolness of delivery that had Marciana purr. Her voice was like a blue flower opening in the room. It had the melancholy grain, Marciana reflected, of a woman arriving at the Gare du Nord to find that her lover has let her down on a still September day.

Marciana never knew when Donatien would arrive and take her by surprise. Her days spent in the sealed and partially restored castle of La Coste were like an extended dream in which her erotomania increased in proportion to her fantasies. She dipped into her excitement with tentative fingers outlining a chasm in which all the tumultuous history of the Sade family burnt like ruins flaming at the bottom of the sea. Each time she touched herself it was like setting the fuses to nymphomania. Her imagination activated her sexuality, and the two combined to create a perversely stimulated eroticism.

Marciana tormented herself with her fingertips. She tickled the circumference of her need, but played at preventing herself from coming. Her fingertips described circular digressions from an irritated clit. She teased herself with exploratory dabs at her eruptive core. She didn't dare allow her fantasies to retrieve Donatien, for he had taught her that the mythos of her back passage contained all the erotic fictions in the underworld. He had made that tunnel his study on a journey to the centre of the earth.

Marciana kicked her legs over her head and arched herself into the posture that yogis call The Plough. It was a position that Donatien loved her to assume. She had changed the CD to Billie Holiday's *Lady In Satin*, and she wished Donatien was there to play her clitoral ridge with a violin bow, and to tune her up before he set about his obsessive preference for putting her end-up on all fours, her hands ritualistically pointed into stilettos that fitted her fingers like red gloves.

She relaxed into Holiday's liquor-grained voice, her intimate phrasing evoking a subtext of personal ruin. Marciana had come to identify with the lives of ruined singers, and to her ear Lady Day sounded so irredeemably sad that she could have been standing singing in the arena of her broken heart, an earthquake arena in which bloody roses poured out of dusty fissures.

Marciana wanted to write a book about fallen angels. All the broken ones: Bessie Smith, Libby Holman, Dinah Washington, Judy Garland and Billie Holiday. She could hear them all crying in the rain. Their tears smudged the windows at La Coste. They were out there in their satin gowns imploring to be taken back into life. They wanted to live and love all over again.

Marciana righted herself, got off the bed, and wearing nothing but her panties, went over and sat on the purple velvet throne that Donatien had insisted be installed in her bedroom. The throne was monogrammed with the ancient symbol of the Sade family, an eight pointed star that had originally been associated with the three magi. The Sade lineage was rich with mystic connotations, and La Coste under Donatien's aegis had become renowned for its sexual rites. Marciana had witnessed how the theatre walls would sometimes bleed in the autumn, and how lines of penitents in chains would arrive at the castle and implore to be granted entrance.

Marciana's world was so hermetically contained by the legendized sexuality associated with La Coste that she had come to live by night in order to enter more deeply into the château's mysteries. For her it was always midnight, and candles and flambeaux burnt in the theatre. Donatien had originally supervised the building of his private theatre, a space that covered a thousand square feet, with a large stage constructed along the northern wall. Marciana liked to sit there in the deep night. The walls were painted cobalt, and the ceilings were frescoed with stars and extravagant depictions of buggery. From the round bottomed belles of the 18th century French court, to the thong wearing supermodels of the 20th century, women were depicted being ravished from behind.

Slipping a full length sequined gown over her black panties, Marciana took herself from the throne in her bedroom to the theatre which lay at the northern end of the second floor gallery. Her staff were asleep. The château was still like a liner on the night seas. But then an urgent and increasingly desperate scale of pleasure reached her from Nina's room. Nina, who had been brought to the château by Donatien was in the process of reaching orgasm. Her pleading cries and throaty entreaties were being answered by an expertise that had Nina scream her volatile pleasure to the silent halls of the brooding castle.

Marciana remembered Nina's arrival at La Coste. Donatien had brought her into the theatre on a long chain, with a shocking-pink bow tied around her naked buttocks. Undoing the ribbon, as though Nina's bottom was a box of chocolates, her brother had placed a red carnation-head in the crack before proceeding to flog his porcelain-cheeked prize. And when it was all over, Nina's exhausted body had been carried to a bed heaped with hundreds of pink and red carnations. Her blood had mixed with the full-throated flowers, and on the following midnight a tattooist had come to Nina's room and needled the Marquis's own symbol of an eight pointed star onto her left buttock. The redoubtable signature D.A.F. de Sade had been inked on to the other cheek.

Nina had proved Donatien's most insatiable convert. It was she who tuned his whips like the strings of a guitar, stretching and coiling their lengths so that they sung on contact with flesh. Nina knew by ear the precise bullwhip that the Marquis was flexing on any captive bottom, and was adept at polishing their handles, and positioning whatever flower had been chosen to sit in the victim's crack. Marciana reflected on how Donatien could cut the head off a tall stemmed carnation protruding from round buttocks at a distance of twenty feet. The whip would slice off the flower with savage precision.

Marciana picked up a torch and carried it over to the stage. It was here that torch singers performed by special request, and here that she and her brother presided over prepared rites at La Coste. Marciana remembered being lifted on to the horns of the stage altar after her honeyed bottom had been dipped into a tub of furry bees. Donatien's whip had quickly laid into the squalling bees, but not before she had known the fury of their assault.

Sitting there in the dark, she was listening for the sound of his boot heels in the corridor. The pale grey leather thigh boots he wore never ceased to excite her by their appearing to be a part of his body. With his three quarter length velvet coat and velvet leggings, and his flame-red hair tied back in a pony-tail, the Marquis struck a presence that was both glamorous and vicious. He would sometimes arrive with two humans on leashes, handling them like someone would recalcitrant greyhounds. At the first sign of uncooperation he would produce the lash. He had quickly taught his initiates to sit under the table like dogs, as he sat sipping a vintage the colour of autumn trodden underfoot in deep woods.

Marciana listened. She was certain a car had drawn up in the courtyard. Donatien's limousine with the blackened windows and the orange satin cushions on the rear seat had no registration plates, and was polished to a gloss each day by a chauffeur forbidden to use any other material but black silk.

And suddenly the corridor was coming to life with his presence. His boots were ringing their staccato arrival, and his indomitable energies could be felt rushing through the vaulted corridors. Marciana felt the excitement communicated to her sexual itch. Her brother contained within him an erotic dynamic that would have brought even an enraged bull to heel.

When Donatien entered the theatre he resembled

somebody who had crossed three centuries without incurring a line. There were no signs of the successive facelifts he had undergone in the course of surviving hundreds of years of being hunted across the face of Europe. He frisked a rhinestoned lead on which a girl with black hair cut straight to her hips was in tether. When Donatien came to a halt she cowered at his side, while he fastened the lead to the outstretched arm of a wooden angel.

He stared long and deep at Marciana, who opened her sequined robe so that her full breasts tumbled into view. By torchlight her eyes looked like a panda's, and she placed her tongue in the hollow of her cheek as a sign that she was ready for him.

Donatien immediately asked for Nina to be brought to the theatre.

'See to it that she's tuned the South African bullwhip,' he said to Marciana in an imperious tone.

'You create permanent night,' Marciana threw back at him, allowing her gown to slip to the floor, as she crossed the theatre, presenting her bottom to him on high heels, as a foretaste of what he would later enjoy.

Donatien sat in a deep velvet chair, awaiting his sister's return. He reflected on how he had christened her Sister Midnight one night in Berlin, in the years when they had travelled together. It had come about due to his having allowed Marciana to be the only woman to have sodomized him, and she had done this with a leopard-spotted dildo, entering him dead on the stroke of midnight.

The next day he had gone out and bought her a black catsuit and a black rose, and after whipping her severely had left alone for Paris.

Donatien was jolted out of his reverie by the sound of two sets of high heels clattering across the theatre's wooden floor. Marciana and Nina walked hand in hand towards him, and Nina who had been dragged from her lover Jacques's embraces, carried in her left hand the prized bullwhip that he had requested.

Nina who was dressed in a floor-length diaphanous negligée approached the Marquis, knelt at his feet, and placed the whip handle in his lap.

'It's tuned, your eminence,' she said, resting her chin on the toe of a polished boot.

'Let me hear it sing in the dark,' he instructed. 'But first of all I will powder Marciana's cheeks.'

Nina handed the Marquis a Guerlain compact, and without waiting to be prompted Marciana bent herself over her brother's lap. With a practised fluency of movement, Donatien hooked down Marciana's transparent panties, and proceeded to dust her bottom with iridescent powder, kissing each cheek after he had perfected the shimmering glaze.

Marciana submitted to her brother's playful teasing by kicking her legs as though she was swimming in heavy water.

Donatien, as a master of restraint, disconnected from the urgent impulse to ravish his sister's bottom and prepared himself to savour the sweet agony of delay. Only later, after he had marked his love, and won from her the approval of suffering, would he begin again his long pleasurable journey to the interior.

Marciana was reluctant to get off her brother's lap. Donatien appeared to be polishing her bottom with the fond appraisal of a jeweller working on a stone. Marciana's buttocks symbolised *la qualité française* to Donatien, a harmonious distribution of gluteal tissue that dictated a shape as perfect as an inverted ace of hearts. Donatien ran a finger deep into the cleft, feeling for the rosette that had become his portal to mystic revelation. That cleft shaped like a circumflex accent in reverse was a dark window giving on to the starry abyss.

Withdrawing his finger and placing it into the perfumed thimble that Nina held out to him, Donatien dismissed his sister with a round slap on her cheeks.

'Show me how your tears will bleed for me,' he said. And like a Daughter of the Precious Blood, Marciana walked towards an altar lit by torches. Photographs of contemporary singers were framed like icons against the altar's backcloth. An androgynous Elvis Presley, a martyred Billy Fury, a drugged and pouting Judy Garland, a feather-boaed Shirley Bassey, a saucer-eyed Dusty Springfield, and a histrionic, diva-like Marc Almond stared out of photographic portraits into the diffused candlelight.

Nina led Marciana to the altar. Her hands were placed in supports under the arms of an angel. Donatien called this prop the Angel of Mercy, for it appeared as though his victim in the act of being flogged, was supplicating for a shelter that was never granted.

Nina slipped down Marciana's panties, placed them in an alter-dish and handed the sacrosanct offering to the Marquis. Donatien responded by kneeling for a long time at the opaque window of his sister's bottom. He knelt there for five minutes in the absolute silence of the theatre, then rose and motioned to Nina who handed him the finely tuned bullwhip.

'Prepare for your salvation,' Donatien warned his sister. 'In the name of the House of Sade you will meet your redemption through the whip.'

Donatien stood back and with an abrupt gesture unleashed a sizzling whipcrack on Marciana's bottom. The echo reverberated like thunder in the vaulted theatre and drew a stifled cry of shock from the victim.

With unflinching composure Donatien issued second and third cuts with a savagery that seemed inhuman.

At the first sight of bloody tears, the Marquis knelt, received a tall-stemmed red rose from Nina, who had removed it from an altar vase, and placing the crimson rose in his sister's crack, he began to pray.

His spiritual agitation was intense. He kissed the flower protruding from his sister's bottom, and called on the abyss within her to reveal its secrets.

That done he stood back from his sister, his eyes fixed

on her bottom. She remained fastened to the angel, as though the two of them had found love on the edge of death.

Nina went forward, prayed briefly to the rose, extracted it, and with trained expertise began applying alleviants to the cuts inflicted on Marciana's bottom. This done, Nina took the bullwhip from Donatien's hand, and presented him with a glass of vintage cellared from the château's vineyards. The De Sade wine was the colour of a black tulip. Donatien tasted the sunlight, dust, sweat and flinty soil of his estate compounded into the grape. Autumn was permanently in his blood. Each time he performed sex rites he would smell dank leaves and rain teeming into yellow woods.

Donatien savoured in the taste of the wine the enormous melancholy arena of his heart. All the grief of the centuries had accumulated there, like thunder clouds piled above a graveyard. The death he had never experienced through the centuries existed as an enigma in his cells, a potential that was still unrealised. It was with Marciana that he shared the secrets of his deathlessness. The cryonic longevity that invested both their lives was a scientific phenomenon that he had begun little by little to impart to his sister.

Marciana was escorted out of the theatre by Nina, and taken to her bedroom to be prepared for her brother's visit. Marciana was to be dressed in all the fetishistic accoutrements that appealed to her brother. She lay face down on the bed and felt Nina's fingerpads work a cocktail of aromatherapy oils into her skin, and very gently into the pouting *trompe-l'oeil* of her rosette. Nina spent a long time working on Marciana's bottom, polishing the curvature of the cheeks, and using an oiled brush on the depilated crack, traced painterly brushstrokes between the abyss and the vault in which it terminated. Marciana's bottom was treated with the reverence afforded a fetish. It represented godhead to the Marquis, and was an artefact that had several times undergone silicone lifts in the interests of acquiring the perfect shape for Donatien's pleasure.

Nina teased the crack with her tongue, and felt Marciana wriggle with excitement. Her job was to treat Marciana's bottom as a beautician would a model's face. Moisturizers were applied to the buttocks each night, and so were depilating creams. Foundations were matched to skin tones and blushers complemented the subtle artistry of bottom *maquillage*. Each night Nina applied an hour's massage and skin-care to Marciana's bottom. Marciana's panties were chosen to represent the colour palette of Donatien's moods. All of them were monogrammed with the Sadean insignia of an eight-pointed star. The penalty for anyone else daring to wear Marciana's panties was to be bullwhipped fifty times by the Marquis, a punishment that Nina had undergone in her initial weeks at the château.

Marciana's bottom, still manifesting evidence of Donatien's savage whipcuts, was sponged with a natural foundation. Its heart-shaped harmonic proportions rose to receive the periodic enquiry of Nina's tongue. The two inverted arcs simmered with expectant pleasure. But Nina was forbidden to enter the rosette with her tongue, and so satisfied Marciana by teasing her with prehensile rimming.

Marciana's bottom was perfumed with dense, nocturnal *Must*, an aphrodisiac scent from Cartier that answered the pungent, autumnal notes that invested the château.

Nina put on a record of the French chanteuse Barbara, and the wavering notes of 'Amours Incestueuses' invaded the room, the song narrating the poignant story of condemned love between a middle-aged parent and a child of twenty. It was a song that they often listened to together as a prelude to the sodomitical incest that Marciana was to undergo.

The two women kissed, Nina's tongue rolling in circles round Marciana's palate, before pushing for her epiglottis. Nina aroused Marciana's nipples, touching them like a pianist hardly stroking the ivories, but rather suggesting a sonata by extra-sensory touch.

Marciana moaned, her body rippling like wind-chimes

in an undulating breeze. Nina could bring her to the point of orgasm by this subtle play of energies, and a partly strangled cry escaped her lips, as Marciana sensed Nina's tongue-point stand on her left nipple with her breath tingling on the surface of the purple areola.

If Marciana hadn't been expecting her brother, she would have called for the bee and honey dip on her vulva. The game involved having her vulva coated in honey, and at a certain point of arousal Nina would release a bee from a glass receptacle, and Marciana lying on the bed with her legs wide open anticipate the insect's attraction to her honeyed spot. The risk of her being stung on her clitoris as a result of the bee's irascible frustration at being unable to free itself from the glutinous honey was the tension that excited Marciana to convulsive orgasm.

Tonight, her request for the game was turned down. It was Nina's job to beautify Marciana's bottom, but to keep her erotic hunger tamed until Donatien was ready to begin his mastery of her bottom.

The castle was so oppressively silent, so cut off from the world, that the two women were glad of the music. It was Donatien's authoritative decree that none of the château's inhabitants should ever leave the fortress's wooded precincts. His abductees were frozen into a time-warp, a trance-state conditioning that held them secure within the castle's labyrinthine complex. And to Nina, who was the most recent of Donatien's captives, the château's complement of slaves resembled drugged noctambulists who only came alive at midnight. It seemed to her that it was only then that they achieved knowledge of their true identities, and with it a regressive awareness of the past.

Nina stood back and reviewed Marciana's bottom. Its shape had been regularly corrected by liposuction, the misappropriated fat removed with the help of cannula tubes. Marciana's restructured prosthetic buttocks were the result of injections with her own fat to create a solid silicone base to the muscle tone. The process was repeated every two to three years, so as to avoid silicone migration, and to ensure that the bottom she presented to Donatien conformed precisely to his demands.

While Marciana lay face down on the black satin counterpane, luxuriating in the massage she had just received, Nina busied herself with the other ritualistic preparations necessary for heightening Donatien's sense of illicit sex.

Nina attended to the massed profusion of red carnations that backdropped the ornately carved black bed. Black altar candles had been lit around a page from *The 120 Days Of Sodom*, copied out in a script that employed gothic majuscules and unicals. Nina would have to operate a camcorder and film the event in close-up, so that no least detail of the sexual proceedings would be lost to the Marquis, whose archived footage proved resourceful to his obsessive need to validate and improve his particular method of sex.

Special condoms monogrammed with black roses or eight gold stars on a black latex background had been placed in a heart-shaped dish beside the bed. Hints of lavender and frangipani dusted the air from a smoking incense cone.

Billie Holiday was singing 'I Cover The Waterfront' as though she had never conceived that there would be an audience for her work. To Marciana it sounded as though Billie was singing to herself in a hotel room, and so giving voice to a grief that had come to possess her over a lifetime, but which had only found register in the moment of its understated release. It was the naivety in Billie's voice in contrast to her seasoned heart, that had it live for Marciana as an instrument of confessional pain. Her voice mixed spring and autumn in one timbral season, and Marciana picked up on its fragile pitch as a pivot on which to rest her sadness at being exiled from the world.

Marciana liked in the deep night hours, as she and Nina sat waiting for Donatien's visits, to tell Nina something of her brother's extraordinary life; and of how he had married

Renée-Pelagie on May 17, 1763, at the church of Sainte-Marie-Madeleine parish in Ville-l'Evêque, already poxed, and bringing his venereal disease to the ceremony. Renée-Pelagie had proved singularly unattractive, masculine, and despite her family wealth, unrefined in her manners.

Marciana told Nina of how she had been separated from her brother at an early age, after Donatien had been caught attempting to saddle her bottom, and how she had been disowned by her father the Comte de Sade, and sent to a reformatory. But no sooner had her brother moved with his bride to the apartment prepared for them on the second floor of the Hôtel de Montreuil on rue Neuve-du-Luxembourg, than he had called for her, and dishonoured the marriage sheets by making love to his sister in the bridal bed.

Marciana remembered too how she had visited Donatien at the Montreuil's château at Echauffour in Normandy, and how she had arrived late one night in the pouring rain, and had met Donatien at a prearranged spot under a large oak at midnight. Marciana told Nina of how she had worn nothing but a pair of red silk panties under her black greatcoat, and that Donatien had conducted her to an outhouse in which there was an old split mattress and hens bickering in the wadded straw. And there they had spent the night together, while the château slept, and the rain had sheeted its brilliant syntax across the surrounding woods. Donatien had ploughed her unremittingly, and his whip-marks had left her skin looking like a matelot's striped vest.

Marciana's memory was a constantly downloading source of Sadean anecdotes. She was able to remember the exact colognes her brother had worn on occasions important to both of them, and the colours of clothes he had chosen to match the big crises in his life. She had been the recording eye visually retrieving the detail that had accompanied the moment. She would tell Nina of Donatien's leg of mutton sleeve silk blouses, a modified style of shirt he still adopted on autumn nights at La Coste. She remembered jackets, coats and boots he had worn in his perverse libertine youth, the old Paris cowering at his feet like a dog surprised by authority.

It was the quiet hour, as the two women called it, the interlude between sex rites when the Marquis prepared himself to consummate incest. It was a space in which Nina too would speak of the life she had known before coming to the castle, and of how she had worked in a bar in Rousillon, a place Donatien had stopped off in on his journey back to the château. His limo had run out of fuel, and he had ostentatiously entered the completely empty bar in which Nina was waitressing, and their liaison had begun with this encounter.

Nina tirelessly repeated to Marciana the compulsion she had felt in Donatien's presence to humiliate herself before his disciplinarian command. He had ordered her to leave her job on the spot, and to come with him immediately to his château. Nina spoke of how Donatien had dog-collared her in the car, and that she hadn't protested for a moment at the leash to which she had found herself attached.

The two women would speak of Donatien's indomitable power, and also of the mystic aura surrounding his person. He had in the eighteenth century presided over numerous public flagellation cults: the Recollects of the rue du Bac, the Daughters of the Precious Blood, the Daughters of Cavalry, and the Grey Sisters from the parishes of Saint-Sulpice, Saint-Laurent, Sainte-Marguerite, La Madeleine and Saint-Germain l'Auxerroi. A galaxy of round bottoms had been bled in the street, and Donatien's spectatorial eye had recorded it all through the fast-tracking centuries. Marciana had never questioned her brother's untiring omnivorous preoccupation with bottoms, and had come to accept this fetish, not as an aspect of his psychology, but as the subjective thrust to his whole being. Presiding over the gluteal choreography of *coitus in retro*, Donatien had according to Marciana found his way to the paradisal city in her rectum.

Nina busied herself with painting her toenails. Midnight

Sapphire. She belonged to the Marquis's private, sodomitical harem, a race of sex-slaves conditioned to obey his every sexual request. She had no way of telling when Donatien would demand her bottom, and so she had constantly to look attractive, should his spontaneous desire demand her favours.

Nina heard his footsteps before Marciana. Her ears were alert to his impatiently assertive step, and sometimes she would hear him all night long pacing from room to room of the dormant château.

When he came into the room, he looked like he had ingested drugs, and he was concentrated on Marciana's bottom to a degree that eliminated all incidentals. His eyes were spaced into sexual trance. He placed the lit torch he was carrying into a holder beside the bed, and began slowly to undress.

He was indomitably erect, and Nina kissed the head of his cock, before applying a star-glitter gel to the prepuce. As a preliminary to entry, and Nina's rolling on one of the Sadean-crested condoms especially manufactured for his use, Donatien would like to tease Marciana by placing his cock along her cleft. He would position it like a guitar-neck on her similarly lubricated crack, and pick out frets of pleasure along the soft lining of her vault. It was Donatien's tuning process, a prelude that would excite Marciana to the point of screaming.

Donatien's penis was jutting out from a pair of Marciana's black silk panties. It was part of the ritual that Nina should tease these off his bottom, after having gelled the tip of his cock. He submitted to Nina's provocative manner of undressing him with an air of passive resignation. It was only with his sister that Donatien gave voice to the excitement that would rage through his body. With any other partner, male or female, he would adopt a role of autocratic diffidence, and appear to be fucking them from the remove of his aristocratic *hauteur*.

Marciana was lying face down, her chin resting on silk cushions, her hands tied, and her bottom raised by the support of cushions beneath her stomach. Her buttocks were angled to ensure maximum provocation. Nina extinguished the cove lights and the room was lit by the single torch that Donatien had placed by the bed. The frescoes on the cobalt walls jumped alive, their sensual morphologies suggesting a correspondingly shaved pubis on the other side of foregrounded buttocks.

Donatien, who derived pleasure from anticipation, withdrew from his foreplay with Marciana, and motioned to Nina that at some stage of the activities, Jacques was to be introduced to the room in the role of dual-fucker. Donatien liked to receive what he was giving his sister, and through being active and passive at the same time, his arousal was intensified. The chain had been known to extend to triple, quadruple and quintuple fuckers, all of whom in their remorseless fucking communicated with the sex trigger in Donatien's brain.

Marciana's bedroom was soundproofed, for her brother fed on silence as a stimulus to his clandestine sexual vocabulary. He would gorge on Marciana's bottom like a snake, knowing that no scream of protest would ever find its way to the château's other inhabitants.

According to a preconceived ritual Nina rolled the special Sadean sheath on to Donatien's tugging cock. The eight gold stars were grouped round the teat, and Nina ran a viperine tongue over the sharkheaded prepuce. Donatien tilted for deep throat, as though he wanted to fill an impossible constriction with maximum input.

Jacques burst into the room with the pretence that the Marquis was under arrest. It was his prerehearsed role to enter on an authoritative note of law, and to bullwhip Donatien if he showed any least sign of weakness in his resolve to fuck Marciana.

Donatien entered Marciana's lubricated rosette with the expertise of a man who over the centuries had accustomed himself to no other form of sex than sodomy. The blind eye in his penis began to open as it penetrated Marciana, and found its pivot in her abyss. From there he could view his past sexual history as a series of insightful footage. He saw himself convulsively fucking a redhaired adolescent in the 18th century in a small house in Paris, while two glowering negro pimps bullwhipped the Madame for some minor act of impoliteness to himself. There had been something about the autumnal streets which led to the closed house that had alerted him to the awareness that one day he would be criminalised for his actions. He experienced it all over again, as his deepening thrusts provoked extended moans from Marciana.

He had known on that afternoon with the redhead that the secret contents of his mind had grown transparent. The big chestnut trees umbrellaed above the house appeared raffishly conspiratorial in bringing his sexual misdemeanours to light. There was a feeling in him that the street had something on him too.

He had reached a brief resting-point in Marciana. He eased his weight off her back, but still kept her impaled on his indomitable erection. She wriggled, making circular motions from her hips as a signal that he was not to withdraw. Donatien felt an excruciating tension in his balls. He felt like he was being tickled by a testicular nest of ants. He knew from the anticipation that when he finally came his ejaculation would be like a solid column of scalding sperm.

But he was still back in a grape-coloured 18th century day. This time it was at La Coste. He had insisted on taking girls and youths from the local village back to the castle. Something about the atmospherics of the place hooked them, the funereal corridors lit with torches, the heavy red drapes and erotic statues, the permanent smell of night that invaded the rooms, and of course his own obsessive, but magnetizing charisma.

That afternoon, three naked men wearing rhinestone crowns had dragged the youths there in a handcart. The men had been whipped up the slope to the château by one of his personal slaves. Donatien savoured the memory of having had the room in which sex took place, sealed up during the time of the activities. Molten lead had been poured into the locks of the fortified door, so that there was no way in or out.

He saw himself again, dressed in purple leather thigh-boots, a purple rinse in his hair, knouting a whiphandle studded with sapphires. He had left supplicant bottoms ridged like tyre-treads. He had waded into the willing in an orgiastic rite in which he had poured bottle after bottle of *Chanel No 5* over used flesh. The dungeon had smelt like a bonfire of scent. Increasingly overcome by a volatile satyriasis, he had carried on whipping until his instruments broke under the strain. The broken handles served as dildos in the ensuing geometry of bodies driven to exacerbation by aphrodisiacs.

As Donatien recalled the brutality of that afternoon, so he reactivated his member in Marciana's subterranean orifice. He dug in deeper. He felt he was releasing stars in her depths that in turn would swim into her eyes. Marciana was the mystic receptacle that gave him life, and he began swimming in rippling undulations along her back. He asserted himself with a lord of the underworld's authority. Marciana moaned as she entered an ecstatic spasm. Donatien pointed in deeper, as Jacques laid a single hot lash across his buttocks. He went deeper still, raiding the vaults of her inner sanctum.

It was Jacques's task to make a liturgical recital of certain passages from *The 120 Days* as the fucking entered continuous deep motion. Donatien was still a long way from generating the eight-pointed star that burst into Marciana's vision at the moment of orgasm. This Sadean manifestation of a supernova was the miraculous sign engendered by their incestuous pact. It brought the three magi back to the château, and so often he found himself the recipient of their presents: a gold Cadillac, a consignment of perfume, or three thousand scarlet roses left in a drift by the main door.

Donatien thrust furiously into Marciana's cleft for a number of tormenting minutes, and then let up for another period of respite. He felt that contained within him was a ferocity in the sexual act that could lead to psychosis. He sensed that if he let himself go he would end up mad at the point of orgasm. He would, like Jim Morrison, break on through to the other side, but Marciana would never survive the ordeal. She would be left dead on the black silk cushions, and he would be faced with having to bury her under a tall oak in the château's grounds.

Excited by the morbid prospect of necrophilic love, Donatien crawled like a grappling combat-creature over the blindside of his sister's body. He wanted to impress on her the inexorability of their union. Nothing could ever break that occult bond. Marciana lived to be punished by his sexual dynamic, and to undergo the vision of an eight-pointed star as she screamed her way to hysterical orgasm.

Donatien worked himself deeper and deeper into his sister's backside, but he was still haunted by flashbacks that had him backtrack to past conquests. His mind was suddenly invaded by Marguerite Coste and Marianne Laverne, two of the women who had brought legal complaints against him for the administration of aphrodisiacs, and deviant sexual practises. It had been pastilles of Cantharides flies that got him into trouble. He had insisted that the women ate a quantity that had resulted in vesical lesions. The trouble that had visited him as a consequence was as big as Africa. He had never succeeded in clearing himself of the charges of poisoning and sodomy. He had been busy at the time supervising rehearsals of *Adélaide Du Gueslin* and *L'Amant Auteur* for performance at La Coste. He freeze-framed his distress in those weeks. It had been the first serious opposition he had known to his despotic ego, and he had flamed with vengeance for the women who had dared obstruct his libertine propensities.

He saw himself again in headlong flight for Venice in the company of his valet Latour. His romantic interlude with his pretty sister-in-law Anne Prospère had been calculated to incinerate any last vestige of remaining tolerance extended to him by his mother-in-law.

As he thought of the outrages he had perpetrated on Anne Prospère, so he deepened his hold on Marciana. Nina intercepted Donatien's wishes by fitting a pair of silk stockings over her fingers and drawing them up her arms. With the expertise of her silk fingers she now began tickling Donatien's balls and the crack of his bottom with her cushioned fingertips. At a sign from him she would have to be ready to pump him with a leopard-spotted dildo, while Jacques in turn sodomized her as part of a deviant triumvirate of fuckers.

Donatien was starting to burn on a slow orgasmic fuse. He imagined angels setting fire to the building, and the ceiling dropping on the sexual participants. He fantasized how they would continue their orgiastic excesses on a flaming pyre. Nothing could ever liberate him from Marciana's bottom. The fascination it had asserted over him for three centuries was inexorable. And each time he entered it he discovered still another concealed passage leading to the big room in which kings and queens sat reading a book of wonders. He fucked harder in the hope of penetrating this mystery. As he did so he felt Nina enter him with a dildo, and knew from her short exclamatory cry that Jacques had correspondingly penetrated her sphincter. The momentum communicated by Jacques to Nina and from Nina to himself inspired him to accommodate Marciana with the vigorous activity for which she was pleading. Marciana had contrived to raise herself on her haunches, so that her brother could view the lugubrious animality of her rotating cheeks. His speed now was vicious as Donatien animated his pelvic thrusts to that of an attacking snake. Nina moved in rhythm with Donatien's salient lead, and Jacques drew cries of pleasure from Nina as he inserted a finger into her vulva.

Donatien fed on the power of dominating the collective sexual thrust. If he stopped abruptly, transfixing Marciana on his bloated need, then he denied Nina the orgasm that Jacques seemed about to activate. It was something he would do with vicious spite. He would have Nina burst into tears with frustration, as he held off from opening still another door to Marciana's interior. Jacques too would be prevented imminent ejaculation by Donatien's bringing his own ascendant to a peremptory halt.

Donatien was beginning to invoke the gypsies of Saintes-Maries-de-la-Mer, who had brought a star with eight golden rays from the East. He called on the princes of Les Baux, and on Balthasar, one of the three magi, commanding that they should be present in his sperm when he came. He hammered hard at Marciana's bottom, who in turn was hoarsely enunciating the extremes of her pleasure.

Donatien could feel the incandescent premonitions of orgasm. It seemed impossible that the pressure in his scrotum would ever find release through the constrictive eye of his penis. And sometimes in the act of coming his pleasure had been indefinitely intensified by what had seemed the impossibility of ever ejaculating his load.

Marciana was beginning to communicate the ecstatic trance-state in which she would receive visions. She told Donatien through her exclamatory moans that the first of the eight rays of the golden star were lighting up, and now a second had appeared, and then a third.

Donatien coaxed his deep inner penetration to maximum sensitisation. To protract the cataclysmic mutual orgasm that they would soon undergo, he tickled Marciana internally with both his finger and his penis. A fourth and fifth ray had come into Marciana's vision. Donatien was so concentrated now on sexual apocalypse that he was detached from the singularly carnal aspirations that were being lived out by Jacques and Nina as they arrived at renewed orgasm.

At a word from Donatien, Nina withdrew, so as to leave him deliriously pacted with his sister. His thrusts were accelerating to a pitch that was so final that they were irreversible, like a train picking up speed across the French countryside. The always inconclusive dialogue he held with

Marciana's bottom, was nearing another mystical terminal. Both he and his sister began to speak out loud in lyric discourse. They were like lovers overtaken with visiting fire, and as the star exploded in Marciana's brain, so Donatien experienced the first jabbing intensity of an orgasm that burnt like supernovae sheeting across deep space. Their united body convulsed in spasms as the House of Sade was rebuilt in her rectum.

When the furious assault has subsided, prayers were offered to Laura, the Laura of Petrarch's *Sonnets*, who had once been married to Hugues de Sade. It was she who had visited Donatien during his insupportable years of imprisonment, infusing his dreams with white light, and appearing to him as an intermediary in his desperate hours. As a sign that she would never desert him, she had left a white rose on the floor of his cell in the Bastille, a flower that had proved imperishable, and one which Donatien kept close by him at all times.

Donatien and Marciana remained prostrate before the torch burning by the bedside. Physically sated, and suspended in a state of post-coital reflection, they appeared in their exhausted awareness to be waiting for a word or a sign. It came in the form of Serge Lama singing 'L'Esclave', a song that Marciana insisted on alternating with the English version sung by Marc Almond. The lyrics that narrated the story of a slave in a byzantine harem, whose secret desire was to become a woman, comprised the ultimate paean to a transsexual ethos. Marciana never tired of listening to the song's instructive decadence, nor Donatien to the lines about being bitten by a serpent's slow attack.

They lay there a long time, assimilating the contents of their mystico-erotic journey, before Donatien went to join a deeper and darker night in the castle's depths. Marciana heard him go towards his secret destiny. There would be big cats at his feet, and the sound of rains falling through all the autumns of the world would temporarily accompany his passage through the dark.

Part II

TORCHSONG EXTRAVAGANZA

The theatre had been prepared for the concert. Marciana anticipated Nicole and Leanda's visit to La Coste, and the singer was due to accompany them in their customized leopard-spotted limo.

Ten thousand red roses had been delivered to the château, as decoration for the theatre, and the entire floor-space was ankle-deep in red and pink sequins. Twenty foot black candles, columnar in width were to be lit as an additional histrionic accoutrement to the performance. Open coffins full of lilies, barbiturates and photographs of Marilyn Monroe had been assembled in the orchestra pit. There were black feathered arrows piercing photographic portraits of James Dean, Jayne Mansfield, Elvis Presley, Billie Holiday, Rainer Maria Rilke, Federico Garcia Lorca, Judy Garland and a whole pantheon of icons who had died early or with their lives still unfulfilled. Donatien's original manuscripts decorated the walls. A red gown worn by Marlene Dietrich was draped over the Steinway.

There was a throne on stage: its use being optional to the singer. The renowned torch singer had been hired at extravagant cost, and was a favourite of Marciana's to the point of her knowing the words to each of his songs. He had been requested to preview a suite of songs written specifically to celebrate the Sadean mysteries. There were three open coffins on the stage full of wads of paper money and this was to be the singer's payment. The hundreds of empty chairs arranged for an imaginary audience were to be occupied by memorabilia jackets once worn by the great Hollywood stars.

Litre size bottles of perfumes by Chanel and Jean Patou were lined up so that the guests could receive exotic oblations. There were whips with jewel-encrusted handles propped against chair-backs, and full-length sequin gowns for the singer's use.

Nicole and Leanda, the occupants of the infamous Pleasure Château were due to be driven to La Coste by their transvestite chauffeur. They would be accompanied by their midget, who served as an erotic *raconteur*, supplying Leanda and Nicole with a narrated compendium of perverse erotic experiences.

Marciana looked forward to the fusion of energies promised by the coming together of two notorious châteaux. Donatien would undoubtedly sodomize Leanda's pet midget, and so give birth to the beginnings of a new legend to be cross-fertilized by the respective households. Like the inhabitants of La Coste, those of the Pleasure Château also lived in a time-zone that was permanent autumn. Neither knew any other seasonal occurrence, but that of the dank melancholy of October rains, the ruin of red woods scarved by smoky fog, and the tonic olfactory satisfaction of a world in continuous decay.

Marciana intended to be carried into the theatre in an open coffin, by four pallbearers dressed in outrageous drag. She had decided to wear a seam-splitting dress cut from pink sequins, and to adopt Marilyn Monroe's provocative trick of wearing shoes with one heel slightly higher than the other, so as to give prominent display to round buttocks.

Donatien had promised a spectacular entrance in purple velvet. He was to be seated on a black horse decorated with ostrich plumes, and to be ceremoniously led to a throne in front of the stage. Any horse droppings were to be eaten on the spot by his attendants.

Marciana prepared herself for her visitors. She injected herself with a slow-release aphrodisiac, and had Nina paint her three inch false fingernails a gloss indigo. She sat on Nina's lap in her see-through panties, while the latter prepared her body with a beautician's eye for detail. Marciana was to wear an indigo coloured wig, and her black lipstick was glammed with a dusting of blue stars.

Donatien intended the concert to celebrate the marriage of La Coste and The Pleasure Château. A torchlit banquet was to ensue in one of the castle's dungeons. The guests, as Marciana told Nina, were to eat off black-bordered plates, and the main course would be served with indigo sauces derived from squid ink. Marciana, stabbing her tongue into Nina's mouth, withheld knowledge of the full courses, but told Nina that dessert would comprise a bottom sculpted out of painted sugar and almond paste and filled with claret jelly.

Nina, who came from a rural village near Roussillon, had never heard of such bizarre confections. She slipped a tongue back into Marciana's mouth, prior to making it up, and swam there like a fish patrolling the parameters of its tank. She could feel Marciana growing sticky through her transparent panties, as though a snail had made tracks on the pink chiffon. Marciana began to grind her crotch into Nina's lap. Nina spread her five fingers teasingly over Marciana's twat, and began to play the frets inside her panties. Marciana threw her head back and responded by convulsing in a paroxysmic cry. It sounded like a nocturnal animal had found its way into her throat, one that had come to slake its thirst in a pool in the hills. Marciana was suddenly nothing but vocables, her scale of pleasure ascending according to the expertise of Nina's caresses. Nina moved her fingers from inside to outside Marciana's panties, and played finger-exercises on the transparent gusset. Marciana sounded in torment, as Nina played a game of administering excruciatingly slow caresses. She worked with three fingers, two fingers, and sometimes one. She polished Marciana's clit as though it was a raspberry she was about to tweak and eat.

Marciana let her head and torso fall back on to the floor, and at the same time her stockinged legs worked their way round Nina's shoulders, and her pussy was presented to Nina's lips. Nina entered it with her tongue like a hummingbird sipping at a flower. She tracked in as a telescoping enquirer, little by little savouring the pepperish glitter flooding Marciana's passage. Marciana was arriving at a state of pre-orgasmic agony. She worked herself harder against Nina's tongue, as though it was the pivot on which she depended. Nina used her tongue like an erect penis to bring Marciana off, the friction invading every centimetre of her erotic core.

Marciana's blue hair poured across the floor as her racked being was consumed by wave after wave of pleasure. Her climax was a hoarse, thrashed out crescendo of throaty entreaties.

The two women relaxed. Nina placed Marciana's wet panties in the chalice, so that they could be offered to Donatien for his ritual gratification. Marciana then slipped on a pair that were clear as daylight.

Marciana was no sooner zipped into her sheath, than news of the singer's arrival was brought to her room. His dressing-room came replete with black slaves and a variety of wines from Limagne, Roussillon, Tenedos, St. Emilion and Valdepeñas. There were rose-coloured pink champagnes, a massive attack of dark red roses, gifts of perfumes and shirts and makeup. There was also a surprise for him in the form of a box marked with the word *Night*. Inside the box, and bound in black satin, was a notebook containing unpublished passages from *The 120 Days* in Donatien's handwriting.

Marciana was told that Leanda and Nicole had been shown into the sumptuous orange velvet sitting-room, where a juniper scented fire had been lit for the arrivals.

When Marciana entered the room, she discovered a midget sitting on the table, cracking walnuts with his teeth, and fuming with ribald obscenities. He was dressed in a scarlet coat blistered with tacky rhinestones. Marciana had an immediate premonition that this was the vermin that Donatien would skewer with his cock on a game platter.

Two stylishly attractive women had arranged themselves like flowers in opposite chairs. The one who introduced herself as Leanda had poppy-red hair, while Nicole was dark and wore black and white Japanese makeup, highlighted by scarlet lipstick.

Both women were so perfectly made up, that Marciana was not surprised to be introduced to Saki, their private makeup artist, a woman whose mask-like face offset a deeply morose sensibility. Sitting poised in a silk micro-skirt and red satin blouse, she had placed a pink carnation in her lap.

Marciana also noticed a monkey sitting in an armchair, and the midget directed his raucous verbiage at the seated creature. To Marciana's amazement the creature was smoking a cannabis joint, and punctuating its inhalations with the reflective pauses of an inveterate smoker.

Marciana felt an immediate sexual attraction to the poppy-haired Leanda, and knew instantly that it was she whose legs she would like to open in an exacting V, in one of the castle's decaying attics. It was there, she decided, that she would give Leanda the 100 orgasms that resulted from Sadean cunnilingus.

Marciana sat in a chair directly next to the fire, and felt her panties shiver across her bottom.

'Coming here is like home from home,' Leanda commented. 'It's only Raoul who had difficulty with the journey. I mean he belongs to another reality.'

'But I know he'll sing well,' Marciana affirmed.

'He'll love the place,' said Nicole, taking in the ceiling frescoes, and the black velvet drapes that waterfalled from orange walls.

'It's the perfect setting,' said Leanda. 'A torchy, gothic construct, in which he can excel.'

'There may be a real funeral also,' Marciana alluded.

'One of Donatien's relatives, an astronaut from the defunctive space-age is brain-damaged from his last return through the re-entry corridor. For years he's lived in virtual space, a hyper-real substitute for his interplanetary missions. Donatien has the idea that as his relative will die a virtual death, so sex after death may biologically resurrect him. It's one of my brother's hypotheses about deathlessness.'

'These things sound rather like our encounter with XZ,' said Leanda, 'the leader of a deathless cult who visited The Pleasure Château. He has the secrets to biogenetic engineering, and he and his android sect claim to have overcome the genetic inheritance of death.'

Leanda crossed her legs in a way that was like a provocative means of origami. The promise in what they concealed was to Marciana like the idea of a flower growing at the bottom of a lake.

The women sat and spoke of new combinations of neurotransmitters, DNA memory banks, and the whole cellular morphology required to create a new species. The need to redesign neurocellular chemistry was a theme of Donatien's, and one that similarly preoccupied Marciana. Organisms in all their complex structures had evolved and stabilized their forms over millions of years, and so too their own deconstructing mechanisms. Marciana was aware that Leanda and Nicole may also have been initiated into infinite life-extensions, and that four people presently at La Coste were faced with the possibility that they may never die.

Marciana talked of her brother's attachment to La Coste, and the blue Luberon mountains which formed a natural amphitheatre beneath windy clouds. Donatien had added new rooms to the château, she informed Leanda, and had also beautified the grounds by planting olive and almond trees. The house had been an obsession of his for centuries, and each detail of change had to be approved by him.

'There are rooms that not even I have entered,' Marciana told Nicole, her eye attempting to telescope up the latter's silk skirt.

'Donatien has forbidden me access to a suite of rooms at the castle's interior,' said Marciana, 'And each time I go in search of them, they appear to be in infinite regression. A few weeks ago I felt compelled to undertake a new journey to try and locate the whereabouts of his secret domain, and I must have fallen asleep in the process, but continued sleepwalking, for at some stage Donatien slapped me awake. He led me back through passages I had never seen before. There were children who opened doors and looked out at me, and their blue eyes seemed frozen into permanent trance. It was impossible to know if they had just arrived, or if they had been there for ever.

'Donatien tried to assure me that I had dreamt of the presence of children, and that what looked like a bottomless hole at the end of the corridor, was simply a nightmare phenomenon. I remember a creature that resembled a jackal snouting at my legs, and the animal wore a collar of sparkling blue stones.'

'It sounds like a journey to the underworld,' commented Leanda, as the midget performed a shoulder-stand on the table.

'You'll meet my brother later,' said Marciana. 'He plans to make a spectacular entrance in the theatre, just before Raoul comes on stage. I don't need to tell you his story. His biography has been made known, although the real Donatien seems always to have been excluded from the story, like the subject left out of a photograph. Only I truly know his story. Sometimes I find myself writing it all down, typing it all on to disc, but without the knowledge of how or when the confessions will ever reach the world. And paradoxically, I suppose he must have known a similar despair when he was writing his huge novels in prison.'

When a transvestite servant entered the room it was to serve a black wine from the La Coste vineyards. The wine had the fragrance of the violet petals in which it had been fermented.

'I have to warn you of certain aspects of my brother's behaviour that may disquiet you,' said Marciana, crossing her legs with the exaggerated slowness of a woman teasing an admirer's volatile sexual appetite.

'Donatien can best be described as an interspecies time-traveller. Naturally, some of the old patriarchal hegemony into which he was born persists in his attitudes, but this has been tempered over the centuries by adoption of very modern ways. And because my brother remembers so much, he is constantly sad. His melancholy is lifted only by his enjoyment in the sexually perverse. You must be shocked at nothing.'

'I have stories that will shock him,' said the midget, disengaging from the monkey's licentious caresses. 'Stories that will bring the stones of this castle down.'

The midget slapped his thighs with gloved hands, his raucous laughter creating a mad happening in the room.

'My brother's aesthetic,' said Marciana, 'has become the substance of legend. One of the reasons he can never die is that he has grown to be a fiction. His life is continuously extensible through narrative. The mystery of Sade is not only in these stones, but on our breath.'

'I can understand that,' said Nicole. 'I once considered myself to be the guardian of an unrelatable secret. I thought I had buried it in my interior, but then I dreamt it, and on another night I spoke it out loud in my dream, and Leanda heard what my dream was saying. And that is how stories begin.'

Nicole was interrupted in her speech by Nina coming into the room in a slinky cocktail dress to announce that the concert would start in fifteen minutes. She poured herself over to Marciana, knelt down at the latter's feet, lifted her stockinged toes out of one of her stilettos, and placed a note in the left shoe. That done, she abruptly left the room.

They could all hear the rain starting up outside, its slow, melancholy elocution drawing increasing attention to itself. The rain was asking to be heard as it fell through the autumnal dark and the oaks that umbrellaed the château's austere watch over the surrounding countryside. It was a rain on the increase, and on the giant video screen monitoring the château's entrance, they could see the smoky columns running diagonal with a wind, a wind that shook the oaks like the props of a low-flying security helicopter.

Marciana marvelled at the indomitable seductiveness generated by Leanda's recrossing her silk-stockinged legs. The perennial sultriness of the *femme fatale* was natural to both these women, and engendered in Marciana a need to discover their bodies as though she was encountering sex for the first time. She could feel the moistness spreading in her flimsy panties at the prospect of seeing Leanda step out of her skirt or Nicole's legs going up high over her head as she positioned herself for cunnilingus from a tongue grained by caviare.

When the party set out through subterranean corridors for the theatre, they were preceded by servants carrying lit torches. They were like a procession headed towards an amphitheatre for the spectacular revelation of mysteries. They walked past cages in which memorabilia was framed. Marilyn Monroe's white panties were modelled by a mannequin constructed to the screenstar's exact statistics. There was a sixties purple velvet suit worn by Mick Jagger and the Mr. Fish dress that he had sported on stage at the Hyde Park Festival in 1969. There were Guerlain lipstick tubes that had belonged to Bette Davis, Greta Garbo and Rita Hayworth. There were whips that Donatien had used in the 18th century, a pair of black brogues that had belonged to Oscar Wilde, manuscript pages from Huysmans's *A Rebours,* a military tunic that had belonged to Michael Jackson, and a great variety of historic celebrity ephemera.

The corridors were hung with heavy black and purple drapes, and there was a smell of autumnal dissolution pervading the whole building. One corridor was papered with python skin and monitors mounted on the walls showed footage from some of Raoul's legendary concerts. He could be seen dressed in a variety of sequined costumes bleeding his heart out on London and Paris stages. The voice resonant with emoted vibrato was blue-rinsing the audience with melancholy narratives of unrequited love.

In one of the theatre's dressing rooms, Marciana was prepared for her entry in an open coffin. Nina touched up her makeup, broadening the lower lip's lipstick line, and using a sparkling dusting powder, contributed a prismatic surface iridescence to Marciana's white foundation. She was laid in the coffin with its purple satin lining, and cut roses were heaped over her body. A lit torch was to be placed in her hand on the entrance to the theatre.

From inside a theatre in which Donatien had contrived so many ritualistic orgiastic fantasies, they could hear the voice of Ruth Etting singing 'Love Me Or Leave Me', as part of the selection of pre-concert torch songs.

The select invited audience, who had all arrived at the château in closed cars, were already assembled in the theatre. The funereal interior was lit by giant torches, and only a single blue spot was trained on the stage. The Steinway had been spraycanned with gold stars and hearts, and looked like an exaggerated Las Vegas funeral artefact at which a mummified Liberace may still have been seated.

Nobody had yet seen Donatien, but it was known he would be last to enter on a black horse. The suspense was electric. There was the feeling that a storm was about to break, its spotlights powering through after circling the countryside all day with twitchy jabs of current.

At the ceremonial sound of a horn Marciana was lifted by four transvestite pall bearers and carried into the theatre. Holding her torch vertical she was carried towards one of the two thrones placed in front of the stage. These seats boasted the lettering DAF and MLM, being the initials for the christian and middle names of brother and sister. Marciana entered to the sound of Shirley Bassey singing 'Diamonds Are For Ever', and coincidental with the song a blizzard of glitter enveloped the stage like a sparkling snowstorm. Marciana was lifted from the coffin's satin interior and placed in her goldleaf throne. Roses were heaped at her feet, and arranging herself in the chair, she crossed her legs with the provocative notion that all the money invested in Wall Street was triangled into her crotch.

The music had changed to Gene Pitney's 'Backstage I'm Lonely', a song indicative of Raoul's predicament in waiting to come on. Most of the audience were dressed in fetish costumes, their clothes dripping with rhinestones and glitter, their makeup comprising heavy eyeliner and black lipsticks. Marciana looked across at a girl with poppy-red hair, who was wearing nothing below the waist except a pair of black silk panties matched with black suede thighboots. The girl wore a cat-like mask, and Marciana was curious to know who she was amongst the distinguished guests invited from the aristocratic châteaux of the South.

Suddenly the whole select audience swung their heads round as the Marquis entered the theatre to a storm of dry ice smokily fogging the entrance. Donatien was visible through the haze in his electric orange jacket, and by the reddish glare of the torch he thrust into the haze. Marciana could see that he was fully masked, and intended to give nothing of himself away to the inquisitive eyes searching his redoubtable presence. He sat polar vertical, all the dignity of his rank contracted into that inflexible posture. He wore the mystic inheritance of the Sade family with invincible pride.

His horse was led by an assemblage of naked slaves, boys and girls who had originally arrived at La Coste as penitents seeking entry to the castle. They all carried tracks from Donatien's whip, but were so compliant to their master, that they would have followed him into the back of a fire.

Donatien's sombrely majestic arrival coincided with the pianist coming out to seat himself ready for the singer's entrance. Dressed in a black velvet suit and a gold satin shirt he took his place at the piano and began extemporizing bars from the introductory number. Marciana thrilled with the anticipation that Raoul was to perform a suite of new songs, written specifically to celebrate and elegize the Sadean mysteries. A mixing-desk copy of the recorded concert would be made into a CD, pressed exclusively for the House of Sade.

Without warning the singer ran on stage, his hands behind his head, and was met by instant rapturous applause. Simultaneous with his arrival under the blue spot, thousands of exotic butterflies were released into the audience. It was a lepidopteral apocalypse, the insects beating the air like ballistic flowers.

Raoul bowed to the applause, threw his head back, then forward again, his torso lit by a mauve-sequined jacket, and followed into a first song that he introduced as 'Sadean Rites'. A slow, elegiac number punctuated by dramatically expressive vibrato, the lyrics evoked a scene in which masked men attended funeral rites by torchlight, and dishonoured the dead by their desacralizing necrophilia. Marciana listened to the hook: 'Under the smoky, tenebrous torchlight/I'll feed on your heart like a wolf/I'm just a sailor whose earrings shine bright/And they mirror the dead eyes of youth.'

When the song ended Raoul knelt in one of the open coffins on stage as a genuflectory gesture to the audience, and in response to rapturous applause threw a number of tall stemmed red roses into the audience. The Marquis got up from his throne, and in unprecedented fashion bowed in the direction of the exultant singer.

Torches were extinguished preparatory to Raoul's second number, a gothic torch song that involved the pianist switching to a Hammond organ so as to evoke the funereal flavour of lyrics sung falsetto, and directed towards a black stained-glass window in which a gold angel glowered. The song exposed the singer's vulnerability as he stayed kneeling in a single red spotlight. The elegy which was called 'Black Hearted Blues' rose in a tremulous column from the singer's phrasing, and related the protagonist's inability to love, and his feeling of short-circuited emotions that inevitably turned love first into indifference, and then into contempt. It was a song ideally chosen for the audience, most of whom were incapable of experiencing love, either due to emotional vitiation induced by excesses, or through dulled sadomasochistic sensibilities. The song quavered into the spotlight's red cone, and seemed in its infinite ascension to rise towards a star. The sonorous overtones established by the Hammond organ provided a gothic overlay to a fragile theme in which the singer hung on to his breath like a spider to a resonant thread.

When the spotlight went dead, the song faded out on organ peals, and the theatre was dramatically immersed in deep night. Again, the applause was tempestuous, and this time Raoul lay prostrate in a crucifixional pose on the stage, arms outspread, and surrendered to a reception that broke over him like fast-running surf.

The torches were re-lit and an additional lighting-rig manoeuvred into place for a song the artist declared to be an exposé of life in a gay-harem. That said, Raoul began by speaking the opening lines of 'The Slave', a version he announced as having augmented with the inclusion of some of his own lyrics. The song was a particular favourite with both Marciana and Donatien, and through its story-line related the transsexual longings of an orgiastic slave to be transformed into a woman. Raoul kept the song's beginnings almost in the pitch of speech, before lifting it from a spoken matrix to the imploring search for death as sexual consummation. 'Drinks of life and drinks of death,' he sang, before taking up position in a cage, and pushing his microphone through the bars as a gesture of defiant liberty. Raoul crouched down with his head in his hands as he prayed to become a real woman. The purple-blue of his indented eyelids was created by spots, and as the song ended so one of the transsexual residents at La Coste danced across stage with all the luxurious abandon of a perfectly created woman. The song faded out with Raoul looking upwards into the lights, as though anticipating an angel's luminous arrival. And to enhance the feeling of ritual death and rebirth created by the song, three figures dressed as menacing crows ran on stage and began to attack the cage with their metallic beaks before being whipped off stage by a scarlet angel.

Again Donatien rose and bowed, his manner suggesting how deeply he was moved by Raoul's interpretation of a song so ideally suited to a performance at La Coste.

There was a pause during which Raoul disappeared into the wings and returned having undergone a costume change.

This time he returned to the stage dressed in a purple satin shirt, and tight black leather trousers. A silver glitter-tear had been painted on his left cheek. The lights had also turned purple, and the atmospherics were pooling for a new song called 'Night In The Burning Heart.'

The singer concentrated, listening for the pianist's cue, his whole body feeling into the latent power within him to sing from the heart. He waited like someone conjuring a flame into his throat, his makeup standing out under the lights. In his posture he represented a wounded diva surrounded by the symbols of love and death. He extended the pause for dramatic effect, feeding off audience suspension, and entered the song as the single light turned from purple to red. What he delivered was a ballad of tempestuous lament, as he cradled an effigial heart needled with pins in his cupped hands, and told the story of a tormented lover who sets fire to his own heart after having dug a grave for himself in a deep forest. When the song concluded, the singer stabbed a jewelled dagger from Donatien's private collection through a red heart, and set fire to it. Red and blue flames jumped into the air, and two naked attendants came on stage to extinguish the fire.

There was a pause in the concert, while the singer went off for still another costume change, and when he returned he was dressed in a gold lamé shirt and black satin trousers. His trousers were tucked into gold boots and stardust had been sprayed into his gelled hair. A giant photographic portrait of Elvis at the time of his rhinestoned Las Vegas debacle served as a backdrop to the singer's moving cover of 'Heartbreak Hotel'.

Marciana placed her hand in Donatien's and felt the cold stones on his fingers. His hand had all the passive assurance of a basking reptile which had succeeded in eluding death for three centuries. He turned her hand over in his as a note of the brotherly affection he felt for a sister who was a compliant sex-slave. Their pubes came together in a complicitous dual affirmation of blood coursing through the Sade lineage.

Any form of touch between the incestuous couple generated a vocabulary of impulsive desire. Each translated the other's need into telepathic discourse. Sitting in the concert they were engaging in virtual sex. Donatien's sense of aristocratic decorum had him give all his attention to the singer, but inwardly he was devising the libidinal geometries in which his sister's bottom was a website of potential whip-cuts.

And Marciana reflected on how the togetherness she shared with her brother was a pact in which continuous desire was stronger than death. One overcame the other in a process of fluent displacement, and in this way they would never die. Donatien's alchemical knowledge of *coitus in retro* generated the serum necessary for uninterrupted life extension.

Marciana looked across at Nicole's right face profile, and wondered if she too would never die, and if the formulaic capsules that sustained life at the Pleasure Château were subject to tolerance. Wouldn't they all disappear one day into a black hole, she reflected, or into a mansion in the sky where the archetypes continued to conduct obsessive fictions?

When Raoul introduced a song called 'Zodiacal Angel', the theatre swam with gold light. Thousands of gold stars rained on to the stage. He had draped a full length star-embossed velvet gown over his gold lamé shirt. Sound effects in the form of the sonic roar of a wind-tunnel served as an intro to the song. The stage changed from the gold of autumn chrysanthemums to a partial black-out as Raoul entered the song from the narrative point of La Coste being a flaming château in the stars presided over by a zodiacal angel. The ballad built slowly to heroic proportions, and the message contained by the lyrics was that of the indomitable power of the imagination to take heaven by storm. The defiant, invincible dynamic informing La Coste would hold a place as a light in the stars. Raoul sang of how 'A burning blue diamond/was the angel's swimming pool.'

The theatre was once again plunged into total darkness, with an intermittent flutter of gold sequins snowflaking onto the stage. There was a sustained pause before a violet spot returned to find Raoul kneeling in front of a heart-shaped elaborately gilded mirror, the frame decorated with cupids. As he sang a lament, 'Creases In The Soul', so he was playfully whipped with tall stemmed roses; the gloved flagellants striking him across the back and shoulders. The three girl flagellants wore nothing but gold angel's wings and white see-through panties. They had been bodysprayed gold, and at the end of the song ascended vertically from the boards through an opalescent dry-ice smoke-storm.

Marciana reviewed the audience again, as Raoul waited for the applause to die down. To her extreme left she could make out a woman wearing ruby sequins, and seated beside her was a panda-eyed man whose irises were lensed silver. Marciana felt a disquieting shiver play the frets along her spine, as she made momentary eye contact with this visitor to La Coste. Marciana remembered the story of XZ's cult, and of how his alumni were identified by silver lenses, and felt apprehensive that her castle had been infiltrated by the alien sect who had placed their inimitable blueprint on the Pleasure Château.

Marciana looked again, and this time the man was

staring at her as though he had found her out. Their eyes had pacted in a way that suggested the alien *knew* her in terms of cosmic identity. Marciana felt she had been seen through, and that a read-out of her reincarnational history was included in the man's insightful knowledge.

Marciana reaffirmed the pressure of her hand in her brother's, and tried to dissociate from the cause of her sudden fear. She experienced a sense of inner disequilibrium, as though a dependable pivot had shifted, and in doing so had caused the misregulation of her mood.

Raoul was taking up with another new song, 'Death Rites', for which he was swathed in black marabou and feathers. The same pall-bearers who had carried Marciana into the theatre, now set about performing the last rites, and Donatien made it known to Marciana that the body they were carrying in the coffin had been dug up from a local graveyard. It had been made up, and dressed in jewels, and would later on feature as a gourmet course in the banquet.

Raoul's lachrymose elegy was for the body of a youth committed through burial to the sea. This blue eyed, blond kid in the song had killed himself on a white beach, and prior to overdosing had covered himself in the star spangled cloak he had stolen from an exclusive store. It was a theme that could have come out of a novel by Jean Genet, and the singer executed it with characteristically heartfelt panache.

Donatien made it known to Marciana that he was going to present Raoul at dinner with one of the emeralds that had belonged to Petrarch's Laura, so impressed was he by the concert. He slipped a hand to the mould of Marciana's skirt over the curvature of her bottom, as though promising her renewed sodomitical ecstasy. Marciana felt her bottom pout in the sultry manners of a woman seeking caresses after an argument over dinner. Her bottom responded to Donatien's moods like a chameleon to the light. It could be flirtatious or occluded depending on how their chemistries interacted. Over the years her sphincter had become her sensitivity gauge, and the muscle had developed an autonomy that dictated her emotional and sexual needs.

Raoul was already announcing that two more numbers would bring the private concert to a conclusion. Assistants came on and brushed up his makeup, retoning the foundation where sweat had made inroads into the white pancake, and with a pencil redefining his lips.

Raoul lit into a penultimate song called 'Love In A Graveyard', the lyrics depicting the lives of sexual outlaws in the smoking ruins: 'Love in a graveyard, in smoking ruins/the redhead carnations/the exchanged assignations/in the ruins before dawn.' Marciana gave herself up to the singer's translation of emotion into crystallized lyrics. The graveyard scene was one that she had experienced with Donatien on innumerable autumn nights. She had regularly been committed to an open grave, and positioned on all fours, her only items of clothing a diamond choker and elbow length black satin gloves, and roundly buggered on the carpet of sedimental leaves that had tumbled into the cavity. Her knees had lost support on the wet leaves, and her pivotal balance had been her brother's insurgent penis. Flashbacks scored holes in Marciana's thinking, as Raoul emoted his lyrics to the coffined body on stage. It was the gravity of the sexual act with Donatien that never failed to impress her. The solemnity of the rites, and the apocalyptic implications of the act had Donatien treat sex as the highest form of mystic knowledge.

At the end of the song Raoul kissed the corpse on the lips as a silent cortege of naked bodies followed the coffin into the wings. The singer temporarily exited from the stage, and was replaced in the immediate foreground by a number of actors dressed as portentous crows, who broodingly hopped about the space that had been occupied by the coffin.

When Raoul came back on it was to announce a last song called 'Blood Roses'. With the stage littered ankle-deep in red roses, and with his pianist dressed in a rose-motifed jacket, the singer, with one arm raised towards the lights, and with his voice pitched to emotional overreach, conjured a pantheon of private heroes on his breath. He addressed Jean Genet and Garcia Lorca, and offered them blood roses for their homoerotic martyrdoms. And of the *enfant terrible*, and his brother in perversion, Arthur Rimbaud, and Paul Verlaine, he lyricized how 'I feel more than certain/your lives knew a moment/outside such long torment/when the fire in your wineglass/was a Spanish sunset.'

The song compounded of romantic realism was a celebratory elegy for the great outsiders whose poetry resonated through the stormy decades as a constant to the anarchic principles of youth. Oscar Wilde made a brief appearance in the song, and so too did the tyrannical psychopaths, Nero and Caligula. The song ended with a storm of roses descending to the stage, and the singer decamping to a standing ovation.

By way of a single encore, Raoul performed a movingly stripped down version of 'If You Go Away', the song having become a torch leitmotif for loss and unrequited love. The singer balanced the opposites of fulfilment and emptiness that occur in Brel's reflective lyrics, and with gestural ambivalence held out one hand and then the other in the attempt to redress the balance. It was a consummate rendition of a song that stretches and contracts according to the singer's aspirations. Raoul gave it his all, and in doing so fed the lyrics with his own subjective biography. He became the song, touching its heart like a lover, and feeling into it as though his redemption depended on its outcome. He let the final phrase hang in suspension dots and bowed himself out of the lights. The pianist sustained the outro, before standing up to assimilate the thunderous applause.

There was to be no coming back for a second encore, as Raoul was clearly spent. The audience stood up, and as was the custom at La Coste, those who wished went on stage and collected themselves bunches of roses from the surfeit littering the boards. Couples were haloed by the intense light emitted by the immaculately involuted flowers. Some of the vermilion roses appeared to be glazed with tangerine on the undersides, so intense was the light they transmitted. The scene was like a flower festival, and Marciana looked up to see a dark-haired vamp carrying a rose in her teeth, while her lover tucked a number of luxurious crimson flowers in each of her violet suede thigh boots.

But Marciana was anxious to leave the theatre. She wanted to avoid re-encountering the figure with silver eyes who she suspected was either XZ or one of his alumni. She bit her nails into Donatien's palm as a sign that she wanted to get out of the theatre, and the crowd immediately parted as brother and sister moved towards the exit with the indomitable power of demi-gods. Donatien threw a glance back and it was like fire running through fields scorched by drought. It was a gesture that proclaimed he was the castle of La Coste, and that he would live as long as it took the elements to erode the last granular speck of his château. His slaves trooped in tow, and the sound of their chains clattering through the castle's stone corridors was the last note that the audience heard of his savage presence.

Part III

THE UNDERWORLD

The banqueting hall at La Coste was sunk into the castle's subterranean depths. It incorporated a performance area in its plan, and lit that night only by candles, and intermittently spaced cove-lights, it could have represented a setting from Donatien's life in the eighteenth century.

The candlesticks for the central table comprised giant pumpkins, slit like human buttocks, and dressed in a variety of see-through panties. There were excessive rose and lily flower arrangements flourishing from open coffins. The hall simmered with the tension of undelivered storm.

Beside each plate was placed a bottle of expensive perfume, chosen by Marciana to suit the individual guest. Each bottle was housed in a miniature black velvet coffin, with the Sade crest stamped on it in gold. There were cornucopias of fruit, the arrangements finished with edible stardust.

In conformity with Sade's mystic cult of discipline, a jewel-studded cross had been erected in the performance area, and a group of slaves dressed in nothing but tiaras and stilettos were awaiting their turn on the cross. It had been rumoured that the Marquis would at some point in the proceedings, demonstrate the true art of wielding a bullwhip. It was well known that few people had ever survived Donatien's ferocity, and still maintained a taste for discipline.

A great fire had been lit in the hearth, and the logs

roared under increasing consumption by flame. The conflagration was massive. It was as though the sun had been set to burn in the voluminous hearth. Naked bodybuilders, their skin glazed with oil, attended the fire.

A strip of purple carpet had been laid across the flagstones, connecting with Donatien's seat at the table. A maid had been selected to brush the carpet as he walked, and there was a personal valet at hand, whose task it was to keep Donatien's makeup perfect. Should a cheek need a little more highlight, then the defect was instantly amended. Donatien as a person, demanded constant and assiduous attention. Any assumed fault in his person would be reflected in a violent mood-swing towards despotic behaviour. His attendants fussed his appearance to the point of obsessiveness. Eyebrow pencils and eyeliners were kept at hand, should a flaw occur in Donatien's *maquillage*.

On a five tiered wedding-cake stand, girls had been arranged in various erotic positions, and were there to be licked, should any of the guests feel inclined to do so in the course of the banquet. The girls wore white bridal headdresses, long drop-earrings, and were all uniformly dressed in white crotchless panties. They mostly sat with their legs wide open by way of provocation, or as additional titillation, petulantly sucked a thumb, or ran a tongue over an upper lip glossed with scarlet lipstick. The blonde prize on the top deck of the arrangement, was busy going through a variety of yogic postures, aimed at emphasising the elasticity of her legs, and the round curvature of her perfectly proportioned bottom. She wore a white see-through baby doll skirt over her crotchless panties, and had her eyes made up like a panda's.

Marciana, leading a panther on a leash, to complement Nicole's leopard, took her brother's arm, prior to entering the hall. Marciana's dress was shockingly tight and transparent, and she wore nothing beneath it, but a black G-string. Donatien had retained the velvet and satin costume he had worn to the concert, and his air of indomitable *hauteur* stood out in eyes that were like frozen lakes.

Raoul and the midget joined the party of guests who included Nicole and Leanda, and a cursory glance from Marciana told her that the silver-eyed man, who she suspected to be the redoubtable XZ, was also in the party standing at the entrance to the dining hall.

As the Marquis, accompanied by his sister, entered the room, so a trumpeter, sporting angel's wings, took up his place on the stage to herald Donatien's entry.

The girls positioned on the cake-stand, seeing the Marquis's entry, all presented their bottoms to his attention, and maintained that position until Donatien was seated. Their crotchless panties were split at the back, so that the arch and the abyss of the buttocks were on view to his eye.

Donatien's seat dominated the table, and at the opposite end facing him, was not a head and torso, but a bottom, chosen as a focal point for its representing *la qualité française*. Working on a rota basis, a series of male and female buttocks would be presented to the Marquis throughout the course of the banquet.

Nicole and Leanda took up places opposite each other; Marciana faced Raoul, and another twenty guests, including the midget and his companionable monkey, all occupied seats beneath the glowering candles. XZ, with his silver eyes, appeared to be everywhere, such was the fascination he asserted by his presence. Marciana noticed immediately that it was impossible to avoid him. She sensed his removal from backside fetishism, and felt resentful at his intrusion into the sodomitical rites at La Coste.

Nina came into the room in a purple PVC dress, and delivered one of Donatien's prize bullwhips to him, so that he could cut at anyone who took his fancy. The whip had been tuned, the way a violinist prepares his instrument. It vibrated like a rattlesnake prepared to strike.

Wines from the vineyards at La Coste were poured, and in the tenebrous light, the guests could feel the oppressive weight of the centuries as they crowded into the hall. The banquet had the air of a ritual conducted in the underworld.

As the Marquis raised his glass to celebrate autumn in its permanence at La Coste, so the first of the oiled slaves was raised on to the cross. The figure presented to the diners was that of a Breton girl. Her whipper began by kissing and licking her bottom in reverence to its harmonic proportions, before he cut a red lateral across the white square. The stroke reverberated through the hall, and was rapidly followed by a second and a third. And almost concurrently, the rains resumed outside in a steady, levelling staccato downpour.

The brief whipping over, a still unidentified guest approached the cake-stand. Bowing to the Marquis as a gesture of respect, he extended a prehensile tongue and flickered it between the crotchless panties of a stormy-haired French belle, who had been busy rolling a black grape over her irritated pudenda. The guest retrieved the grape with his agile tongue, swallowed it and returned to his seat, leaving the girl in a state of raging torment. She scissored her legs wide, and by way of invitation to the hall, ran her five fingers over her clit, like a guitarist fitting a plectrum to taut strings.

The blonde prize from Toulon, who commanded the top deck of the stand, began to roll on silk stockings with the finesse of a trained stripper. And after having secured the stocking tops to suspenders, she began easing the gossamer-fine silk back down her thighs, over a bended knee, and then sheer off twitching toes. She undressed her right leg, and then her left, and lay back, legs arched open, languorously awaiting the first of the guests who would claim her on the summit.

As an afterthought to her stockings-strip, she took the dark rose from her bridal head dress, and placed it between her legs, as though a petalled mouth was exploring her white crotchless panties.

As a first course, the guests were served quails, each with the head tucked under one wing. The course was preceded by a cocktail – two parts brandy, one part calvados, one part sweet vermouth, known at La Coste as a 'corpse reviver'.

It was Donatien's nature to express a sense of bored disrelish with all food. As an inveterately jaded gourmet, his tastes were awakened rarely, and then only by a dish so extreme that he would savour it more as a curiosity, than as something contrived to bring him gustatory pleasure. Instead, he concentrated on the corpse reviver cocktails, imbibing each bittersweet drink with the reflection of a man tasting his infinitely extensible biography.

Marciana and Raoul entered into enthusiastic conversation about aspects of singers for whom they nursed a corresponding passion. They spoke of Nina Simone, Jacques Brel, Scott Walker, Barbara, and of Billie Holiday and Elvis Presley. Marciana was a completist, and was exceedingly knowledgable about bootlegs, rarities, collaborations, and all the items of an artist's work that go to form a complete collection. Marciana also collected memorabilia, and was proud to own black silk panties worn by Billie Holiday, a cache of postcards that Elvis had scribbled to friends during his army years, negligées worn by Brigitte Bardot, stockings that had breathed on Monroe's legs, sunglasses that had belonged to Scott Walker, and a whole wealth of memorabilia.

Marciana told Raoul of how sometimes she would put on a pair of Billie's black panties, listen to her latenight music, and have Nina undress her with her teeth over a period of hours. By that time, she told Raoul, her panties were so wet that Jacques had to be called for to fuck her to the point of screaming.

Raoul expressed his own fetish for drag-clubs, and thick cocks under tight little skirts. He asked Marciana if she could procure him a pair of Elvis Presley's Y-fronts, a trophy for which he was willing to pay a lot of money.

Marciana maintained an animated front of conversation with Raoul, and then with Leanda and Nicole, in the hope of excluding the weirdo with silver eyes who would periodically spook her by directing his eyes at her body. She sensed it wasn't the sexual stare of a man appraising her curves through a transparent dress, but more the detached scrutiny of someone observing her as a cryogenic exhibit. Marciana had the feeling that the man saw right through her into the archetypal contents of her psyche. He appeared unnatural to her, to the point of being a walk-in – one of the many extraterrestrial infiltrators who touched down in order to transmit data back to their particular planets. She knew intuitively that his sort of sex would be head-games. She drew up a picture of him as a mind-fucker, a being who would sensitise the limbic area of the brain, and orgasm in his head like an adept of Kundalini.

Wine was being poured as a postscript to the lethal corpse revivers, and at the far end of the table, a woman dressed in a red micro-skirt was down on her hands and knees ingesting her partner's cock. She played with it like soluble asparagus, letting the heavy head rest on her lower lip, while her tongue circumambulated the triggered girth.

Marciana pointed out to the interested midget, that this woman, called Lorraine, actually ran a smart school in fellatio. Pupils were taught how to suck cock, and comprised both women and gay men. Taught initially to suck on dildos, pupils then graduated to the real thing, and enlisted models lay prostrate on beds, sporting huge erections, and verbally encouraging the pupils in the arts of deep-throat, cheek repository, lapping, licking, tonguing the frenulum, and other forms of cocksucking extravaganza.

Marciana informed Raoul that Lorraine's clients included everyone from princesses to prostitutes. They were educated in how to play the cock like a wind instrument. The erectile nerves, Marciana explained, were treated like finger-stops, and the anatomy of the penis was studied as an aid to understanding its potential for pleasure. Alumni of the School of Fellatio, were considered like Lorraine, to be so expert that they could blow a man if need be in two seconds, or over two dilatory days.

According to Marciana, Lorraine was soon intending to widen the academy's study to take in cunnilingus as a complementary subject. At dinner parties Lorraine liked to dress and cocksuck like a scarlet slut. She would eventually, Marciana warned, make a circuit of the entire table, and reward all the men present with the tormenting expertise of her deep-throating prowess.

Having unsatisfactorily picked at a quail's wing, Donatien declared himself ready for a first go at the exhibits on the cake-stand. At a peremptory sign, the young French girl he had chosen, presented her bottom to the divine Marquis, and he, without removing his gloves, appraised its curves. He appeared to be weighing her buttocks in his hands, and then polishing them, like a masseur rubbing oils into the body.

He did no more than that, certain in his mind, that he had claimed his first sodomitical prize for the night. He liked to be excited by a variety of bottoms, before he fully entered the mystic rites of his sister's passage.

The assembled guests eagerly awaited a second course which was described in the personal menu as Soles In Coffins. A melange of jacket potatoes in béchamel sauce, two fillets of sole per person, plus half a lobster cut into half-inch pieces, the latter having been poached in white wine, was to be served with the potatoes cut into coffin-shapes.

Marciana could hear Nicole and Leanda eagerly discussing what they called an itchy-panties technique of excitation, with a vampish diva, whose mouth was bruised by a definitive black lipstick. Nicole was describing how she would fill a pair of Leanda's favourite see-through panties with a deliciously ticklish irritant, and Leanda would go through minutes of wrigglish ecstasy, before a rapaciously tormented schoolboy was introduced into her bed. He had first to remove her ticklish panties, place some of the aphrodisiacal irritant on his prepuce, and then begin the solid fucking for which Leanda was by this time, desperate.

For all her initial aversion to the weirdo with silver eyes, Marciana knew deep down in herself that an encounter with the man was inevitable. She had ascertained from Nicole that this figure was indeed the redoubtable guru XZ, whose teachings had brought to their Pleasure Château, the knowledge that there was no need to die.

Marciana assumed that XZ would be anxious to psychically decode Donatien's knowledge of cryogenics. Both châteaux were in possession of the secrets of virtual biology, and Marciana wondered if their medical data intersected. She was already aware that any attempt to seduce XZ would prove impossible, and that contact with him could only exist on a mental level. She fixed her eyes on him, and instead of averting his as a signal of non-aggression, he continued to stare at her with imperturbable menace.

Donatien idled with the second course. He offered a forkful of sole in béchamel sauce to a redhead from Bordeaux, sitting open-legged on the second tier of the cake-stand. She nibbled at it, letting her saliva escape into suggestive tears. But Donatien wasn't sufficiently aroused to want to bugger her. He fed her a second forkful, and then sat looking at the lobster on his plate with the disinterest of a man surveying a mortuary. He segmented the perfumed flakes, and let them individually settle on his tongue, but he still lacked any form of focused appetite. All he could think of was his sister in her transparent dress, and his inordinate desire to re-enter her sphincter.

Marciana was feeling correspondingly in need of being fucked. It was only with her brother's insatiable penis rooted in her interior, that she felt complete. She savoured her food with the appetite of an adept at French kissing. Her eyes were like a cat's, as she delayed the passage of lobster into her throat. When she lifted her wineglass, it was as someone who tasted the centuries in the sensual fermentation of the grape.

A lively conversation had opened up between XZ and his patrons, Leanda and Nicole. XZ was discussing the reality of spacecraft being fuelled by solar-powered xenon-ion propulsion, a means of efficiency he was describing as specific impulse, compared with brute force chemical rockets. He was imparting to Nicole the technological infrastructure of why chemical rockets used thousands of pounds of propellants, whereas the ion engines consumed no more than 80lb of xenon.

XZ had estimated that such a craft would enter a 200-mile by 22,000-mile geostationary transfer orbit around Earth, and that the weight saving would allow the craft to be used to carry a bigger scientific payload or to give the spacecraft a longer life. Firing continuously for 4,000 to 5,000 hours, he explained, would increase the craft's velocity gradually to 25,000 mph, the escape velocity needed to overcome Earth's gravitational influence and travel out into the solar system and into deep space at high speed.

Marciana was aware immediately of XZ's formidable knowledge of space travel and of interplanetary communications. She could feel a schizoid happening in her erogenous zones. While her anus remained the sacred prerogative of her brother's, her pussy felt intimations of arousal at XZ's weirdness. Marciana liked his slim body, and the impression he gave of expansive cerebration. She found herself wondering about the possibilities of his possessing a penis. She couldn't quite decide if he, as an android, would be devoid of genitalia, or equipped with a formidable prosthetic device.

Marciana found herself shivering each time Leanda or Nicole arranged a silk-stockinged leg. The ripple ran through her like wind imparting filigree to a lake's still surface.

An androgynous young man a few places away from Marciana, had taken up a long pink feather, and was busy imparting ecstasy to one of the crotchless-pantied girls on the cake-stand. The girl had succeeded in somersaulting her legs backwards over her head, and was purring with pre-orgasmic pleasure. The exhibit was miked-up, so that the guttural vocables which escaped the girls would be relayed around the hall. The girl ascended a scale of pleasure that deepened to hoarse entreaties. The young man continued to pick at his sole and lobster with the fork in his right hand, and administered his teasing measures with the other.

Marciana was beginning to decipher the names of other guests at the table who had been invited from the Pleasure Château. There was a man with green lenses, who appeared to be inseparable from an imperturbably reserved individual with steel-blue hair, who she noted was called John. The two men preserved an intimacy and confidence that worked to exclude the rest of the company. Both men spoke quietly, a habit accentuated by their manner of leaning towards each other when speaking, as though they had reason to further exclude the chances of being overheard.

Marciana felt marginally disquieted by this couple. While she readily warmed to the feline eroticism emitted by both Leanda and Nicole, she instinctively withdrew from the quasi-human qualities that seemed to belong to the male inhabitants of the Pleasure Château. She could envisage herself eating a cocktail cherry from Nicole's pudenda, or being licked on all fours by Leanda, but her libido went cold at the idea of fellatio with the midget or XZ.

The midget was attempting to entertain his immediate neighbours with a coarse repertory of erotic stories. He was, in between pyramidal stackings of his fork, telling the story of a man who could only come if he was dressed in a *frou-frou*, and spanked with a pink ballet shoe. According to the midget, the man was over another's lap, receiving his delicious punishment, when the mistress of the house returned. Her jars of expensive moisturisers were scattered across the sofa, having been used as part of the fetish, to give a beauty treatment to the man's bottom.

The mistress of the house, claimed the midget, who professed to have observed the whole scene, was dressed in leather hotpants, and feeling frustrated by the failure of her boyfriend to keep an afternoon rendezvous at the Ritz. She apparently said nothing, stripped to her black silk panties, and demanded that her bottom be given a facial. Both men had worked oils into the curvature of her cheeks, before she had demanded from the man whose bottom was already oiled, a cheek-rubbing orgasm. Bringing her bottom into friction with another, by rotating it on the oiled surface, had driven her to a rapturous climax.

Marciana connected with fragments of another narrative, in which the midget was relating the story of a wealthy countess in whose service he had been, prior to taking up his position at the Pleasure Château. The Countess, according to what Marciana could construe of the midget's raucous tale, had a predilection for garage mechanics. She liked their hands and faces to be blackened with oil, and demanded that they shouldn't wash after finishing at the garage. Her powdered body would be arranged, legs open, on white silk sheets, her skin rippling to engage with the oil-blackened youths that she so desired.

The midget, who was into his second plate of lobster and soles, was unable to articulate the whole story, so preoccupied was he with cramming delicate food into his mouth.

Donatien, who was still holding off from the exhibits in their crotchless panties, was beginning to engage in a tentative discussion of cryonics with an equally hesitant XZ. The imperiously aristocratic and the invincibly transcendent met as the differing energies in the two men, in something solid like a columnar flame.

XZ was telling Donatien of high-tech gadgets that enhanced awareness of dreaming. He was talking of the NovaDreamer, a combination of eye-mask and circuitry designed to help the individual monitor his dreams. The wireless NovaDreamer, XZ was explaining, determines when you are in REM sleep, by scanning the patterns of your eye movement. When the gadget judges that you are about to enter REM sleep, XZ pronounced, then it gives you a variable light-

and-sound cue that acts as a mental alert to tell you that you are dreaming – without actually waking you. Marciana could hear him expounding on the high-tech aspects of the NovaDreamer, and how it featured a built-in dream alarm that wakes you five minutes after each dream so you can write it down. With practice, he was saying, you can begin to control the autonomy of your dreams.

Donatien expressed some minor interest in the US-designed Zyberfantasy Sex Machine, equipped with a VR headset and tactile sensors, in which visits to a model in a selective sexual orientation offered auto-erotic gratification.

But Marciana could hear XZ enforcing the notion that spirituality was an essential part of all psychological development. He was talking of the strict meditational practises employed by his deathless cult, and of the need to fuse bioengineering with enhanced psychic awareness.

Donatien, who maintained the glacial *hauteur* associated with his mystic and depraved lineage, was busy advancing the idea of physiological-sites in the brain for longevity implants. Like XZ, he was as yet prepared to give no ideas away about his discoveries relating to DNA, and cryonics. He discussed with XZ the neuroscientific claims of the brain being divided into three segments. Donatien was reminding XZ of the reptilian brain as the site of survival behaviour, the palaeomammalian which corresponds to the limbic system, and the neomammalian which resides in the neocortex. The complex interaction between the three brains, allowed Donatien to believe in locating a channel in the limbic system that would provide uninterrupted sexual fantasy. It would, he claimed, be like watching a mini-TV screen activated by nerve-cell connections in various psychomotor regions.

On a different plane, Raoul was telling several admirers about the vicissitudes he had encountered in a tour of the major Russian states. He was talking of the absence of vegetarian food in depleted restaurants, and of the primitive technological facilities in the theatres at which he had played.

He had carried his own suitcases on to planes, been hassled by border police, but adored by his audience. He had, he said, taken sequins to the Soviets, and intended to do so again.

Marciana saw a switch come on in Donatien's brain, as he abruptly got up from his seat, took his redoubtable bullwhip in hand, and approached the cake-stand. The girls were quick to present their erotically vocabularized bottoms, and Nina, anticipating Donatien's intent, quickly placed the head of a rose in the most inviting cleft. Donatien's aim was rapid like the cast of a fly fisherman. A whistling sizzle, amplified by the mikes, resounded savagely through the immediately silenced hall. Nearly all of the assembled company knew of Donatien's legendary status as a whipper, but none could have imagined the ferocity of his hand. He whipped with the peremptory finesse of an undisputed master. A second and a third cut followed like machine-gun fire, and abruptly as he had risen, so the Marquis sat down and resumed his conversation.

XZ was visibly disconcerted by Donatien's brain-stormed behaviour, and he noticed the speed at which the Marquis resumed his impeccably formal demeanour. It was as though Donatien had dissociated himself so entirely from the incident, that it might never have occurred.

It was Nina's task to climb on the stand and rub emollients into the bottom of the girl who had been so unsparingly thrashed. Donatien busied himself with drinking a glass of vintage to celebrate his unparalleled expertise as a whipper.

The company were so visibly shaken that it was a time before they resumed conversation. The girls reverted to their open legs position, and slowly the hall came alive with the bee-simmer of animated discourse.

Marciana surmised that this halcyon interlude would soon be destroyed by Donatien's insatiable thirst for the whip. She knew only too well, that once her brother's impulses were lit, he was unlikely to be contained by this one outbreak. The exhibitionist in him demanded attention, and the confrontation between a bullwhip and soft flesh, was his assured way of attracting a spellbound audience.

Conversation was suspended by four of the kitchen staff transporting an open coffin through the hall. Steam could be seen escaping from the interior; and the menu prepared for each guest told them that they would on the coffin's arrival be listening to music from *Cantio Ad Laudem Cantioris*, from the liturgical chants of the Aquitainian repertory. This in turn was to be followed by an adaption from the anonymous composer of *Le Recueil Des Plus Belles Et Excellentes Chansons En Forme De Voix De Ville*.

The black majuscule lettering in the menu stated: 'We will be eating the body of Jean Testanière, formerly in employ at La Coste, and born at Oppède. The course is optional. The body is glazed in a sauce of blackcurrants and armagnac'.

The coffin was deposited with great ceremony, but none of the guests apart from Donatien and the midget expressed any interest in the notion of cannibalism. They concentrated on the Vaucluse wines from the Sade vine-yards, and the autumnal tang contained in their mellow notes.

The girls on the cake-stand were being fed delicacies by the guests at table. John, and his friend with the green lenses, could be seen offering black grapes to a kittenish redhead from Marseilles, whose small, button-like mouth promised the constrictive ecstasies of fellatio. She would lick the escaped grape juice from the corners of her scarlet lips with the prehensile dabbings of her explorative tongue. Another girl was having the soles of her feet tickled by a pink feather.

Donatien had the glazed corpse removed from the table. Neither he nor the midget had done anything but test the blackcurrant veneer with a fork. The Marquis had other things on his mind, like arresting the secret from XZ that contributed to longevity at the Pleasure Château, and of proving his whiphand in the orgy that would follow on from the banquet.

When the dessert was served, it comprised Crimson Tart in the form of sponge cakes with a sauce prepared from blood oranges, grated lemon rind and cream poured over them as a suitable condiment. Each tart had been pierced with a black love-heart on a stick, and there were bitter chocolates in pink foil for the girls on the cake-stand.

Donatien stood up, thanked the assembled guests from both châteaux, and gave a short reading from *The 120 Days Of Sodom*. In order to impress on the guests their security within the walls of the castle of La Coste, in its turn an invitation to engage in every form of sexual licence, the Marquis reminded the company of the redoubtable impregnability of the Château Silling in his infamous novel. He read out the passage about the topographical inaccessibility of the Château Silling to potential intruders.

'Having passed the village, you begin to scale a mountain almost as high as the Saint-Bernard... Five full hours are required to reach the summit, and there an accident in the form of a crevice above sixty yards wide splits the crest into northern and southern peaks, with the result that, after having climbed up the mountain, it is impossible without great skill, to go back down it. Durcet had joined these two parts, between which a precipice fell to the depth of a thousand feet and more, by a fine wooden bridge which was destroyed immediately the last of the party had arrived, and from this moment on, all possibility of communicating with the Château Silling ceased...'

The Marquis put his book down at this point, and was answered by an antiphonal explosion of champagne corks. The bottles had been assembled on the mini-stage, and now exhaled a plume of smoke impressive as any dry ice special effects. Donatien had given the signal that for as long as the guests were at La Coste, they were free to engage in every form of sexual fantasy.

Raoul was called to the stage to perform everybody's favourite, 'The Slave', and positioned amongst the smoking champagne bottles, he agonized his way through a histrionic rendition of the decadent lyrics. He sang the song acapella, placing emphasis on the semi-spoken parts, and concluding with a genuflecting prayer to the god of transsexuals, remained head bowed to the boards, as the applause broke over him in voluble waves.

Champagne, again from the vineyards at La Coste, was poured smokingly into glasses. Magnums were placed on the cake-stand, and the girls began the process of intoxication that would lead to erotomania. Donatien, who was notorious for his laboratory of aphrodisiacs, would later on spike the drinks with stimulants calculated to induce nymphomania and satyriasis in the company.

The guests savoured their Crimson Tart, while Donatien again endeavoured to strike a note of enquiry into XZ. He realised that to decode this man's complex psycho-logical structures would demand a mind-bending subtlety, not in any way contingent on sexual liberty. Donatien sensed XZ's predominant asexuality, and the transcendent plane to which the latter aspired. He knew that there would be no easy way to access the man's interior selves, and to hunt out the required formulae from the information highways in his brain. The man clearly existed on various levels of meta-intelligence, and was as much an adept to cyberspace as he was to the occult lodges of spiritual energies. He manifested no interest at all in the beauties in crotchless panties, who under the influence of champagne were beginning to kick their long, nyloned legs in the air, and to stretch them vertical, as though stressing the axis on which they should be fucked. XZ's disinterest in the proceedings appeared to be tempered with a sense of supercilious remove. Donatien's only knowledge of the man was that he was at La Coste as the spiritual adviser to Leanda and Nicole. As he understood it, XZ was working at retrieving both women from a strictly perverse carnal plane, and at resituating them in a more spiritually evolved cosmos. Marciana had told him that both Leanda and Nicole had gained additional life extensions from their android guru, and had incorporated his knowledge into the deathless lives of those who inhabited the Pleasure Château.

XZ had been discussing with Raoul the concept of surgical streamlining involved in cosmetic surgery. He was telling Raoul of the body's tolerance to bioengineered skin, and how almost any biological material can be coaxed from a laboratory culture dish. Raoul, who had a pathological fear of aging, was listening to XZ's claim that living protheses were being developed for every organ system in the body. 'There are civilizations,' he was saying, 'in which even brain cells are cloned, and bioengineered as replacements for expended cells.'

Raoul's vanity appeared consoled by the notions of cosmetic streamlining, and XZ promised to send him details of the best cosmetic surgeons. Donatien decided he would address the issue of multiple civilizations, in the hope of breaking into XZ's psychic database. He wondered if there was a connection between the extraterrestrial cloning of brain cells, and XZ's apparent knowledge of deathlessness; and if one was contingent on the other.

Already, the young androgynous man who had been orchestrating a feather to the considerable delight of the redhead on the cake-stand, had clambered on to the artefact, and was giving assiduous cunnilingus to the object of his desire. He was to be seen using his tongue like a dessert spoon between the redhead's invitingly open legs. After several minutes, the two contrived to achieve the backward 69 position, and the entire length of the young man's penis was soon buried in the girl's accommodating epiglottis. The amplified sounds of their mutual sucking were circulated round the hall as an excitant to arouse the guests who were still busy with the Crimson Tart and champagne.

Without any hint of warning, Donatien picked up the guffawing midget, placed him over his lap, and slapped a plate of cherry tart on his scrawny bottom. That done, he playfully collared him, and lifted him on to the cake-stand, where he was left to be the spectacle of the shriekingly amused guests. And as if to enforce his draconian authority as lord of the château, Donatien brought out a newly tuned bullwhip, and lashed the midget's tart-stained buttocks.

Again Donatien resumed his seat with the circumspect reserve of an aristocrat, and took up conversation with his immediate neighbours, commenting on the autumnal clarity of the wines, and of the immaculate Laura, related to the Sades, and illustriously immortalized in Petrarch's *Sonnets*.

Nicole and Leanda looked scandalized by Donatien's harsh treatment of their pet midget, but were prepared to put it down to ludic impulses inspired by the occasion. The two women had evolved to the sophisticated exploration of extreme erotic refinement, and had little time for Donatien's exhibitionist mania. It was to Marciana in her see-through dress, that they directed their attention, their eyes sitting like buttons on her purple areolas.

They engaged Marciana in reminiscences of the disco diva Dalida, who had died from an overdose of barbiturates in 1976. Nicole, who had experienced a sexual liaison with Dalida, recalled her ostentation, and her popularisation of everything from Courrèges white space-age boots to silver sequined gowns. Dalida whose friends had included Brigitte Bardot, Charles Aznavour, François Mitterand and Johnny Hallyday, demanded her lovers bring her roses and lingerie each morning. Nicole remembered the coruscating diva sunning in nude panties on her Montmartre balcony, and actually sitting on the wrought iron balcony railing, so that opportune passers-by and motorists would catch a glimpse of her back or front in her flesh-coloured panties. Dalida would drink champagne out of a glass prepared with rose petals, or hire a street urchin to paint her toenails green, Nicole was recollecting, or pay prostitutes by the hour to divulge the complex gamut of their dungeon experiences. Three of Dalida's lovers, Marciana divulged, had shot themselves through the head, the last of them being Richard Chanfray, the

Count of St. Germain, with whom Donatien had practised various mystic rites at La Coste.

A number of guests had prematurely left their seats, and were on the cake-stand, involved in an elastic geometry of oral devotion. Torches had been lit to add ceremonial grandeur to this orgiastic prelude, although it had been made clear in the menu that fucking wasn't permitted in the banquet hall.

Donatien who had not removed his gloves through-out the meal, contemplated his wine glass like a jeweller scrutinising a ruby. Nina was fastidiously touching up his foundation, and erasing specks of cobalt mascara from the dusting powder that sparkled on his upper cheeks.

The guests were due to adjourn to the theatre, where cognac and liqueurs would be served; and where liaisons could be struck up, and a harem of girls and boys be introduced as a foretaste of pleasure. But prior to this happening, Donatien decided to try once more and establish inroads into XZ's mental defences. He viewed the man's taciturn alienation with disrelish, and was determined to enter him like a computer virus.

XZ looked with disdain at the young man eating the redhead's pussy like tropical fruit. The girl was instructing the man how to orchestrate her clitoris, and her mouth was open in a rictus of ecstatic pleasure. Donatien fantasised about entering the young man's behind, simultaneous with him licking the redhead's volcanic clit, but he dismissed the idea as a cliché, something he would have done three centuries ago. He had moved on from there in his ritualized sodomitical journey to Marciana's inner sanctuary, and dismissed the fantasy as juvenile.

Donatien could hear XZ talking to Nicole of the concept of a body lacking the events of death or of birth. His was a journey towards desomatization, and the replace-ment of the physical with a form of astral virtual reality. The disinherited body would be the site of neurological implants, and the periodic replacement of dead brain cells by their cloned counterparts would establish a blueprint for eternal man.

Donatien synthesised the contents of XZ's conversation in this way, and listened to his particular terminology, which incorporated words like cyborgasm, robotopia, mutated nucleotides and infobots. The man's techno-mystical restructuring had provided him with a post-biological vocabulary. His ideas interfaced neurology with cyberspace.

'Bodies reconstituted as information floating in data banks can have a profound impact on physical bodies in the real world,' XZ was telling Leanda, 'and are in themselves the impulsed apotheoses of cyberspace.' XZ went on to expatiate about abstract representation of the self and the body, and how greater freedom in the theatre of everyday life can be obtained once the virtual theatre is infiltrated.

Donatien held off and listened to XZ's neutrally delivered encomiums on techno-biology. He realised instinctually that XZ's android physique was dependent on much more than the accoutrements of cyberspace. There was a spirituality to his biomechanical genre which suggested an affiliation to occult orders. For all his speculations about interfacing peripheral nerve axons and integrated circuits to individual nervous systems, the man was additionally informed by the spiritual.

XZ had already sensed Donatien's intentions to break into his knowledge banks, and was clearly resolved to give nothing away. He took a dark blue capsule out of a star-shaped pill container, and swallowed it without ostentation. It was also a gesture of his separation from the progressively coked guests.

Marciana knew only too well that XZ was named after the capsule that he and his initiates had taken in order to transcend genetic death. She knew the story of the Pacific beach happening in which five men and five women had realised what appeared to be immortality of the body, through the taking of a particular chemical compound. Marciana suspected the pharmaceutical aspect of the event to be false. Either that, or the capsules would prove redundant to anybody outside XZ's exclusive cult of initiates.

Donatien sensed that it was the wrong time to engage XZ in a discussion pertaining to the hermeneutics of life and death. He would invite XZ to the luxury of his private rooms in the castle's subterranean interior, the following day. The sexual buzz in the air suggested he go play as an aperitif to the liturgical rituals that would later accompany his taking Marciana to the master bedroom. He had arranged that the whole assembly would be lined up to view her perfect bottom as he escorted her to the permanently sealed doors of his castle sanctuary. But for now, he stood up, offered his sister his arm, and to the accompaniment of servants and slaves, was ushered to the theatre in which he had staged so many scandalous plays.

Part IV

THE HAREM

'Did I ever tell you,' said the midget, ensconced on a cushion by the central fire, 'the story of Lavonia and her chauffeur?'

Donatien suppressed his irritation at the wizened homunculus's intention of seeking centre stage in the theatre, and left him to address a company warming themselves with cognac and the first explorative caresses that would lead to rampant sex.

The monkey, wearing a red jacket raindropped with rhinestones sat at the midget's feet lining and snorting cocaine. Instead, Donatien settled back into a burgundy coloured velvet armchair, and cradled a three centuries old crystal glass tinctured with a measure of benedictine. He listened to the midget wheeze out a salacious narrative, and admired him for his temerity in daring to speak in such formidable company.

'There have never been bottomings like it,' said the midget, 'and all of them with her husband listening outside the door. What's more, they never knew he was a silent voyeur, who after having fed his jealousy with sexual torment, would then go and fuck his brains out at a brothel called the Palais De Muncha. Almost every other afternoon, Lavonia and the chauffeur would get down to it in her bedroom. I had the job of sprinkling drops of Chanel No 5 on her silk stockings and Janet Reger panties. Anyhow, her chauffeur was a right knicker fetishist, and he'd insist on scoring her panties as a reward for

Sister Midnight

the pleasure he imparted to her back passage. The chauffeur would always be in a cap, and wear suspenders and stockings, largely because Lavonia liked to hear the sound of her three inch nails making ladders in his nylons. Each time she made a tear in his stockings, she would come. And each time he laddered hers, his fucking would stampede. She'd deliberately purchased an old mattress from a bordello, so that the broken springs creaked with every thrust. Her husband would be outside the door with an erection touching his stomach button. Sometimes he'd bring a whore in to suck him while he listened...'

Donatien was partially amused at the story's lack of daring, and enjoyed the prospect of watching the other guests ingest substances, while he remained lucidly in control. His erotological vocabulary, he reflected, would prove indecipherable to his uninitiated guests. He would spare them a journey through the château's depths, for he had decided that they would be horrified by the spectacle they would observe. All of the Sadean menagerie of freaks were concealed in the dungeons. Some of them had been there for centuries, and comprised a gothic tableau of catatonic hybrids with a vampirical taste for blood, and an exemption from time that had them appear to be permanently awaiting release.

Donatien knew only too well the advantages to be gained by keeping his private mythology secret. It was his obsession that nobody should ever gain from his weird energy sources. His nuclear family he had decided, would remain stuffed in his vaults.

The midget had abandoned attempts to draw attention to himself, and now sat drinking copious amounts of brandy. Donatien observed the unsubduable egomania that drove the Pleasure Château freak, but let his feelings of hostility go.

Marciana was excited by the angle at which Nicole had arranged her stockinged legs, the intersection of thighs occurring at a point which just edited out the gusset of her panties. The provocation was executed with a feline sultriness that had Marciana marvel at the seductive powers of femininity. Leanda too had contrived to strike a leg pose that was electrifyingly revealing. The latter would periodically take out a scarlet lipstick, and re-establish the arched flourish of her matte bow.

In a flurry of girlie gestures, the girls from the cake-stand came in to mix with the guests. Dressed in diaphanous white robes over their crotchless panties, they playfully sat on laps, and the blonde, called Claudia, was enjoying having her conical breasts tickled by a man and his girlfriend. He could be seen caressing Claudia's right breast, while his girlfriend dabbed at the left with circular pouts. The redhead had formed a definite liaison with the androgynous young man, and was lightly tracing a painted fingernail over the contours of his straining penis. She refrained from unzipping him, and instead teased him through his black satin jeans.

There were bodybuilders attending the fire, and John and his companion with the green lenses appraised their musculature, and were evidently intent on fucking them in the ensuing orgy. One of the girls was at request sitting on a man's face, while a second one was expertly giving him head.

Donatien made a sign that the harem were to be introduced, although he continued to express disinterest in every form of provocation on show. He appeared like someone constantly looking at another time and another place. Nina was in attendance on him, and had provided second and third whips for his relish as the orgiastic imbroglio deepened. The girls kept away from Donatien as though they were skirting a fire. He had no interest in their generous breasts and round bottoms. They offered the sort of sex he had left behind as a boy in the eighteenth century. He had eyes only for Marciana, and derived pleasure in keeping her apart from the incipient orgy. His delight was in frustrating others who would have liked to gain her constrictive rosette. Donatien's eye searched only for potential flagellants, and at the sound of the approaching harem rattling their ankle chains, he expressed his first proper interest of the evening.

An exotic seraglio of rent boys posing as pashas, and Eastern girls wearing sequined G-strings and six inch heels, entered the theatre to the heralding note of a trumpeter. Some of the boys were in handcuffs, and the girls wore ankle-chains trimmed with pink marabou. The boys had feathers arranged in their bottoms, in the form of black and purple plumes, and all were new to Donatien in the hope that he would be stimulated to whip them with resounding expertise. It was known to his staff how quickly he tired of a bottom, once he had marked it with a bullwhip, and so procuresses had been at work for weeks in the neigh-bouring towns selecting penitents for the château. They were to receive the highest rates of pay, but were refused any rights of complaint should Donatien work himself to a state of sexual dementia in administering discipline. The choice was theirs, and so was the possibility that he would make no selection at all from the recruited harem.

It was the young men in whom Donatien expressed spectatorial interest. There was a transvestite in glitter makeup, who possessed the curves usually associated with a girl's bottom, but Donatien disapproved of his pedestrian genitalia. He decided to make no purchase on the boy, but for good measure stood up and executed a stinging lash to the boy's buttocks. It was an arbitrary and random cut, and Donatien looked unsatisfied by his capricious outburst. He withdrew to his chair, determined to preserve his whiparm for the right subject.

The guests were busy making selections from the voluptuous harem. The girls had been taught to wiggle with a circular rhythm that distributed body weight in constant oscillation from left cheek to right. They walked from their hips, and the boys had learnt a similar method of attracting backside attention.

XZ had removed himself to a corner of the room and was sipping at a bone-dry champagne. Donatien felt himself being observed and prickled at the suspected intrusion.

Unable to restrain his insurgent need, the young androgynous man had mounted his redhead, and was vigorously fucking her on a mauve velvet sofa. One of the oriental girls from the harem had presented her backside to the young man, and periodically he would look up from his smouldering redhead, and lick the other girl's pussy. To augment the undulating geometry established by this triumvirate, one of the rent boys began sucking the androgynous young man's balls, while a fifth entered the rent boy, and became the pivotal support for this multiple chain.

Seeing an immediate opportunity to indulge in a little Sadean perversity, Donatien rose, took his marksman's aim at the fifth man's oiled bottom, and struck a blow so severe that the ricochet was felt by everyone all the way down to the impaled redhead. Donatien cut a second and a third stroke, before retiring to his chair. The spectacle didn't merit a staccato thrashing, and Donatien was still intent on reserving his energies for the right erotic construct. It would take a particularly complex assemblage of bodies, or just the right harmony to the proportions of an individual bottom before he would be tempted to lacerate his victims with renowned fury.

Donatien resumed his seat directly opposite, but a long way removed from XZ. The latter's silver lenses were fixed on him with all the inscrutable alienation of an android. Donatien wondered if XZ inhabited the same time-zone as the other guests, of if he lived permanently in what ufologists called missing time. He seemed absent or too present, and Donatien couldn't decide into which category XZ fell. He had the feeling XZ was psyching his impulses, and hoping perhaps to place a glitch in his electrics. He suspected their mental combat would be mutually devastating, and potentially annihilative. But for the time he reviewed XZ from a suitable distance, and admitted no concessions to his intense scrutiny of both himself and his sister.

Marciana had decided that she would definitely go for

a threesome with Leanda and Nicole. The two women corresponded to her feline characteristics, and were inveterately fetishistic to the point of having rhinestones hand-sewn on their panties by one of their Japanese maids. They had been informing Marciana of these details, and of how the two of them owned over five thousand pairs of panties, each garment having been made to meticulous specifications. Silks and transparent chiffons were matched with contrasting lace in the design of the items, the fabric being later finished with pearl or rhinestone decorations, or trimmed with fur or braided sequins. The two women promised Marciana a gift box of Pleasure Château lingerie, describing how each item was monogrammed with the intertwined letters L. and N.

In return, Marciana promised to show the two women her lingerie collection, famous for its backless Sadean panties, and a collection of hand-embroidered silk and satin suspender belts. Marciana was busy imagining the luxurious hours ahead with the three women all modelling items of her lingerie, a thrill that would heighten her own future contact with the garments.

The quintuple of orgiasts assembled on and around the sofa, had been joined by another three participants, two men and one of the harem girls, and they soon contrived to fit themselves into the chain of interactive fucking. The ramified extensions corresponded perfectly to Donatien's idea of sex. It was only in his relations with Marciana that he asserted the prerogative of monogamy. In all other respects he believed in numbers at the expense of couples, and in exhibitionism at the expense of privacy. He sat watching the assortment of harem bottoms like an eagle on its spacey crag. He signalled to three of the boys to present asses, and insisted on inspecting their buttocks from a point of close-up scrutiny. His eyes sat on their flesh like molten drops. He appraised every centimetre with a knowing that had explored and entered tens of thousands of bottoms over the centuries.

After minute inspection of each of the boy's bottoms,

he dismissed them with a hard, disdainful slap. Two red spots glowered like rouge on the bottoms at hand, and Donatien signalled for two Persian girls to come and sit on his lap, something they did by placing their backs to him. He attended to nothing but their blueblack hair, delighting in its texture, the rhinestones sprinkled in the curls, and the perfume with which it had been scented. Stroking a woman's hair encouraged aspects of tenderness in Donatien, and for a moment his psyched up person entered an emotive space, and he was temporarily lost in his absorption of beauty. He liked Marciana's hair to be cut into the sharp definition of a fringe, so that it could be left down, pinned back or swept up in a punky quiff.

Donatien dismissed the Persian girls, and found his eyes jumping to XZ's indomitable lenses. He resented feeling under scrutiny in his own house, and sensed that wherever he sat in the theatre, the visual attack would follow. Instead, he let the wine he was drinking evoke autumn, and imagined boars crashing through moulting forests, and heard again the interminable rains flashing through umbrageous oaks. Part of him would like to have been out riding through the woods, his mind full of nothing but the scent of rotting leaves, and the sound of chestnuts crashing out of high crowns.

Almost all of the harem were now participating in the sexual rites that had begun with the redhead and the androgynous young man, and spiralled into a highrise of undulating bodies, polymorphic pacts and lesbian trysts on human furniture. The redhead had graduated to being used three ways, and her insatiable need pleaded for progressively severer treatment. The orgiasts were creating a synthesis of rhythmically discriminate fucking, and Donatien was quick to note the select number of guests who had refrained from becoming participants in this tentacular syntax of bodies. He observed how Raoul and the midget chose to keep apart, as did Leanda and Nicole, and the increasingly withdrawn XZ. The midget maintained a constant discourse with his monkey, and the two incongruous beings seemed to Donatien's eye to exist on a level of amused harmony. The monkey perfectly understood the midget's raucous banter, and the two of them were busy sharing a joint.

Donatien had decided that his only means of presentation to XZ was to establish a meeting for the following day. He took himself across the theatre, and formally arranged with XZ that they should meet in the library at noon the next day. Donatien's offer was greeted with acquiescence by the expressionless android who sat with a glass of mineral water at hand. And for the first time in centuries Donatien experienced a feeling of disquiet at the possibility of someone possessing a superior psychic power to his own, and with it the potential to raid his memory bank.

He returned to his conversation with Marciana, and explained to her that he hoped once again to meet Laura at her interior, and to engage in a dialectic with her soul. He told Marciana that his penis was the instrument through which the eye of Shiva opened and disclosed a mystic all-seeing in the act of sex. He intended to extend his colloquies with the numinous Laura, and at the point of orgasm to see the heavens open. Donatien claimed that the visionary ladder could be ascended through tantric sensitisation, and that brother and sister would be married in heaven at a certain orgasmic pitch. Their art was to achieve a sustained resonance through which this ecstatic objective could be attained.

The condominium of bodies was beginning to form splinter-groups and some of the split-offs were being led by guides with torches through the labyrinthine corridors that connected with the bedrooms. But a central column of fuckers remained, and the redhead was the pivot on which they depended. She was attempting to engorge a triumvirate of cocks, as well as contriving to form an elastic entry-point for various anatomical fetishists who favoured the helix of the ear, and the warm repository of the armpits. The androgynous young man was sitting out from exhaustion and enjoying having his toes painted by one of the harem beauties. His fingers were being done in scarlet, and his toenails lacquered black.

Donatien surveyed the satelliting orgy-groups with an increased sense of boredom. What he saw was the limitations imposed by physical apertures. There weren't sufficient entry-points in the body to satisfy the complex metaphysics of his anal fantasies. It was the opacity of bodies that had him want to whip them into the representation of distorted forms, or substances re-shaped by the whip. He felt outraged by the prospect that anybody should elude his whiphand. True illumination, he reflected, could only come about through the relation of whipper to whipped. If the initiate was receptive to realising vision through pain, he found himself advocating, then the person could be thrashed to their senses. He felt like flogging the entire company, and awakening them to the ecstatic pain attendant on algolagnia. He saw his whip as representing a short fuse to the collective mains.

Donatien relocated Laura in his life. He owned the copy of Francesco Petrarca's edition of Virgil, in which the poet had written: 'She was taken from the light of day while I, alas, was in Verona, ignorant of this stroke of fate... Her most chaste and very beautiful body was laid to rest on the day of her death, April 6, 1348, at vespers.'

To Donatien Laura represented a vision of the most immaterial, idealized, and diaphanous kind; a passion that found its one consummation in vision. For Donatien, as for Petrarch, Laura was a symbol for amorous meditation. The daughter of Audibert de Noves, she had married Hugues de Sade at the age of seventeen, and Donatien's research had led him to believe that Laura belonged to the circle of educated ladies who made up the 'Love Court' of Avignon.

As a prelude to his lovemaking with his sister, Donatien recalled again how Laura had come to him wrapped in black crepe, and with her blonde hair floating stormily free. She was the white lady of his dreams, and if at times he contemplated defacing her image, by ripping off her black negligée, and imagining in the process her compact buttocks, then he suffered for the temptation. It was the tension contained by the erotic within the spiritual that heightened Donatien's pleasure in his incestuous relations with Marciana. It was Laura who he expected to find at Marciana's interior.

Donatien sat in abstract contemplation of these things, his mind hooking at sacralized and desacralized images of Laura. He had come to think of her as the celebrated saint of the Sade legend, and of Marciana as the living manifestation of the ancestral cult. He had for a long time formulated the idea of marrying his sister, and he intended on the last and third night of his guests' sojourn at La Coste to announce news of the marriage. Donatien conceived of the union as bringing still another scandal to the Sade lineage; a prospect in which he delighted. He would have his bride dress in a sheath of dark ivy leaves, and her hair and veil would be decorated with black roses. He could see her in his mind, standing in the chapel, shivering in a transparent black gown, while castrati celebrated the profane union of brother and sister.

When he shifted from his reverie, Donatien noticed that Leanda and Nicole had gone over to sit with XZ, and that the three of them could be observed in philosophic discourse. The midget was lying face down at the foot of a quadruple sex act, licking a girl's leather thighboot. Three or four members of the harem were attempting to attract Donatien's interest by presenting their bottoms, and he motioned to them that they were to bend over, two on each side of a sumptuous armchair. Donatien received his whip from Nina, and cut into the bottoms of the two on his near side, surveyed his work by how the lacerations coloured, and then went round to the other side of the chair and administered the same brutal punishment to the other exposed flagellants. Again, he watched the blue and red horizontal cuts bump up to rich berry colours, went back to the other couple and delivered a repeat performance. He kept this up for another five minutes, and then returned to his chair. Donatien's obsessive concern with numbers reproduced itself in the lateral cuts he inflicted on bottoms. He had counted every lash he had delivered over the centuries, and the total amounted to more than twelve million. An increasing discrimination over the quality of bottoms to be whipped had considerably curtailed his quota in recent years, and Donatien was now selective to a refined degree over the numbers he selected for disciplinary purposes. He had hopes of achieving a round thirty million successes before desisting from his mania, and was determined over the next days to indulge in some indiscriminate whipping, so as to increase his figures by another ten thousand.

Donatien regarded Marciana's bottom as too precious to whip in any serious manner, and several strokes were regarded as sufficient to stimulate his passion. This minor defacement of her buttocks assuaged his instinct to desacralize beauty. Donatien thought of this act as similar to holding a thorny rose-stem, while inhaling the flower's scent. For him, it was the intoxicating marriage of pleasure and pain that fired his nerves to excess.

With the idea of increasing his total, Donatien took aim at the central body of orgiasts, running in towards it and wielding a quick fire of whistling blows. The attack was sudden and without warning, and the Marquis resembled a dervish as he lived in the ecstatic dementia of the act. He seemed to have overtaken himself, and to be the composite projection of his shadow as he slashed to left and right and back and front of the collapsing construct. Most positions were crumbling like meringue as Donatien ran in a circle round the still interlocked bodies professing his legendary status as a whipper. He was for a moment like a tiger spreading panic to a number of feeding zebra. And as abruptly as he had begun, so he stopped.

Donatien walked back to his chair like a somnambulist. His body was stiff, and he appeared to be in the process of returning to himself from a long way away. He threw his bullwhip on the floor for Nina to lovingly retrieve. She took care of the whip, and began slowly to massage Donatien's neck and shoulders as he regained his composure. He stared ahead of himself as though he had just navigated a re-entry corridor, and called for Marciana to come and sit on his lap.

Marciana wiggled across the theatre in her see through second-skin dress, and playfully teased Donatien with the circular motion of positioning on his lap. He immediately came alive, and ran his hand the length of her thigh, while her black lipsticked mouth responded by kissing him deeply.

'We'll go out to the woods tomorrow,' Marciana said. 'Just you and I. And we'll pick up acorns again, and you by looking at them will transform them to gold. You've always done that for me.

'Will you take me to the woodsman's hut in the oak grove? The place where you sat as a child and listened to the autumn rains. We played there together. You and I heard the acorns and the chestnuts falling with the rain. I can still hear that sound every time it rains. I want you to re-live childhood with me. It all started then for us. We'd take those silk sheets into the hut and huddle under a red cloak. Let's remember those things.'

Donatien looked away into the distance, and smiled. 'I can see it all,' he said. 'Nothing is forgotten. The smell of leaves and horses and leather. Your nipples were the size of hawthorn berries, and your skin tasted of blackcurrants. Do you remember how we wanted to run away and get married? And now we can realise that fantasy. We will be married in the chapel where Hugues de Sade is laid to rest. At the sight of our betrothal he will rise. We will take him back into our lives in the château.'

Marciana looked like she was dreaming with her eyes open. It was her way to enter into whatever world Donatien imagined. His imagination was the bridge she used to span the rainbow. She would sit on his thoughts, as though she was riding a horse across country.

'Yes, we'll be married,' she said, as though it was something she always knew would happen. She expressed no surprise at her brother's decision to marry, but acquiesced fully in his plans to unite their lives in the medieval chapel to the sound of an Aquitainian mass.

'I want you to place a ring on my finger in our old hut,' said Marciana, 'in memory of a childhood that has never died. I hope there will be jays and crows as witnesses of our undying love.'

'Our pact will be an eternal one,' said Donatien. 'Begun in your bottom, our marriage will end in the stars.'

'I can hear the rains now,' said Marciana, 'and they will continue through to our meeting in the woods tomorrow. I want to walk with my face up to the sky, and have my body flashed by the rain.'

The romantic in Donatien could only be touched by his sister. He broke the head off a vermilion rose at hand and offered it to Marciana's lips. He broke off a second one and placed it in her lap, and then a third and fourth were inserted one into each shoe. Marciana luxuriated in the gifts of lipstick-red roses, and expressed her felinity by purring as Donatien stroked her thighs.

'I want you to wear ivy leaves in your hair, tomorrow,' said Donatien. 'And for our marriage, you will have a G-string made from the darkest ivy leaf cut from the château's walls. Nina will have it sewn on to a purple string, and in addition I wish you to have a purple ivy leaf tattooed on your crotch.'

Marciana rippled with acquiesence at Donatien's suggestions. Her body went through the sinuous affirmations of a pond chiming with raindrops. She longed to be moulded to his body in eternity. No other man could hold out any interest for her, and like her brother she viewed the orgiasts with a degree of contempt for the limitations of their sexual pleasure. Their orgasms to her mind would short-circuit in frustrated nihilism. They would never know the march on the mystic interior that Donatien achieved with her in his sodomitical lovemaking.

Donatien continued to cover Marciana in red roses, spiking them in her hair, and crushing the petals into the palms of her hands. Both were conscious of XZ's inquisitive lenses focused on their withdrawal from the other orgiasts.

'This castle is the physical shell of our bodies,' Donatien confided in Marciana. 'When we die, the walls and the roof will collapse. The vineyards will revert to dust and stone. The people here will be fucking in the middle of a wasteland.'

Marciana said nothing. She lived inside her brother's impulses, and lived only for that. His assertions were her truths, and his body an extension of her own. She was looking forward to the hour in which they would retire to the master bedroom, and begin their way of fucking to know visionary truth.

The savagely whipped orgiasts had reassembled into a nuclear force, and this time the nymphomaniacal redhead was clinging to a man's back, while a duet of female lovers licked her clitoris. The young androgynous man had recovered enough of his sexual energies to be buggered by a member of the harem. He found himself replicating the ecstatic measures of orgasm that only thirty minutes ago he had been imparting to the redhead. He had switched roles from active to passive and was in the act of finding the one as pleasurable as the other. To Donatien it looked as though the young man had become the redhead, and was learning through the experience what it was like to be a woman.

The sexual proceedings were temporarily interrupted by the arrival of drinks and chocolates said to incite aphromania. There was also a dish of Crème Fouettée à la Rose, a whipped cream delicacy with an infusion of essence of roses. Strawberries shaped like buttocks had been placed on top of the cream, and the exhausted orgiasts were glad to disengage from their complex geometries, and stop for food. There were cakes studded with miniature choux-buns and pistachios, and filled with macaroons and strawberries.

Donatien delighted in these delicacies, and knew only too well the potency of the aphrodisiacs prepared by him at La Coste. It was the injudicious use of aphrodisiacs on Easter Sunday, April 3, 1768, that had got him into so much trouble with Rose Keller, who he had picked up in the Place de Victoires. He let his mind regress three centuries, and isolated the image of himself in a grey frock coat with a muff of lynx fur. He had been standing with his back to the grillwork at the base of the statue of Louis XIV, when he had seen Rose Keller leave mass at the church of the Petits-Pères, and so it had developed. He had he remembered, taken her to a small house in rue de Lardenay, where two other prostitutes were waiting, and there got into trouble through the liberal use of aphrodisiacs on a woman who resisted his sexual advances. It was all part of a biography he had transcended, but the incident had made considerable inroads into his life, and had contributed to his long years of incarceration for sexual offences. He would never forget Rose and her aggrieved German face, and her testimony outlawing him as an unnatural.

The centuries had developed with him, Donatien reflected, and so many street drugs had come to be used as sexual stimulants, that the use of aphrodisiacal compounds were no longer considered exceptional. But his were unnaturally potent, and as he savoured the first of the pastilles, so he was aware that within thirty minutes his already volatile penis would be rigid against his stomach-button. He wanted to watch how the orgiasts would be affected before he withdrew with Marciana into a sumptuously prepared bedroom.

Most of the participants were busy enjoying the Crème Fouettée à la Rose, and Donatien delighted in the knowledge that they would be little suspecting the sexual irritation that would occur to their genitalia in the coming hours. Donatien enjoyed the idea that the redhead would become a tempestuous nymphomaniac, greedy for every penis that would enter her three orifices. He would observe the considerable fucking as a spectator, while the itch mounted in his cock like lava rising to erupt from a mountain. Donatien liked to savour the growing suspense and irascibility of his semen. He liked his libido to be at the point of detonation before he began the long journey to ejaculation. And even on the point of release he would repress orgasm, and coax the concluding force two or three times to a near head before finally coming. Part of the thrill, he reflected, was in imagining release, so that when the escalating pressure finally exploded, it was because it could no longer be contained.

Wines and champagne were being served, and so too were the best fruits glazed with alcohols. The whole sensual spectrum of the libertine was being observed, and Donatien was careful to see that every detail of the aesthetic was explored. There were oils, perfumes, and emollients, and on one side of the theatre a rail on which a great variety of fetish costumes were available to the participants.

The midget was sitting on an oriental woman's lap, having his tufty hair stroked. The monkey played at his feet, and would occasionally slap the bottom of a girl within easy reach. Donatien and Marciana were joined in a conspiratorial overview of the re-uptake of the orgy, as a number of guests reassembled in a manner that was like ivy climbing one of the castle's walls. They spread over each other in arrow formation, clinging to parts of the body with the tenacious climbing grip of dark liana.

Donatien could sense that the stimulants were taking effect, for the eagerness with which the couples took up with each other again was immediate and devoid of temerity. Donatien noticed that XZ had decided to leave, and he cut a lonely figure in his silver boots, as Leanda and Nicole walked with him to the exit. His hair was tied back, and to Donatien he resembled a post-biological being, a sort of android who had brought the knowledge of extra-terrestrial worlds with him to this planet. Donatien was preparing in his mind for the chance to crack the man's secrets the following day, while preserving the formula that allowed him and his sister to enjoy a longevity that had endured through the centuries.

Leanda and Nicole had disappeared with XZ into the recesses of the château's corridors, and Marciana felt anxious lest she should be denied the women's favours. Marciana had been inwardly preparing the erotic configurations she would enjoy with the two women. In her mind she knew their lovemaking would be exhaustively beautiful, and that in terms of oral expertise they would enjoy a prerogative that no man could ever emulate. Their combined tongues would reach places that she suspected men never knew existed. All the little millimetres that formed the circumference of the clitoris were to Marciana the most exquisitely sensitive of places, and were part of an erogenous dynamic that men in large neglected. It was a part of the body that she liked to make up with lipstick, thereby eroticizing the clitoris as a woman's central point of focus. Marciana looked forward to the careful application of red or black or mauve or shocking pink lipstick points to Nicole's clitoris, and to propping Leanda up on all fours prior to writing obscenities on her buttocks with the same lipstick.

Massive, anatomically incongruous fuckings were beginning to take place, and two men had contrived together to enter a woman from behind, and had both been penetrated themselves by another two men from the harem. The quintuple effort of the orgiasts was volcanic, and they moved around the floor like a weird sea creature, a mollusc on ten legs that was straining to find an axis, and which fucked itself into awkward motion.

To Donatien the exhibit looked like something escaped from the sea-bed of Lautréamont's *Maldoror*, and he allowed the orgiasts time to establish a pleasurable rhythm before cutting at them with a whip. He administered only one searing cut, and the noise describing the whip's trajectory was like that of a stick jumping out of a fire. Donatien stood back and reviewed his work, and the two men who had taken the ferocity of the blow were marked with lateral stripes. It was a cut with which Donatien was pleased, and he went forward and examined the wound and ordered a photograph to be taken of it, and had Nina video the weird conglomeration of bodies, all irritated to the maximum degree by potent aphrodisiacs. Donatien realised that even if he should lay into them with multiple strokes, they would maintain their erotic positions, so urgent were their needs to continue fucking.

The divine Marquis felt a gold autumnal halo surrounding his whiphand. Whenever he was most alive to himself, this aura appeared. He knew it as a sign that he was on the road to mystic vision. He was certain too that his marriage to Marciana would be another stage on the road to apocalypse.

Elsewhere in the theatre, groups or couples were singularly devoted to establishing geometries of sexual pleasure. Two of the oriental women were sitting facing each other, legs arched, and were tickling themselves to orgasm with the use of long feathers. Most of the girls in crotchless panties, who had been liberally revealing themselves on the cake-stand had been taken away to the bedrooms. Donatien imagined them being bounced hard on the creaky springs of the château's beds, beds he had purchased from brothels, and which had seen endless service from hungry sailors in Marseilles. He himself had pinned redheads in glassine stockings to the bordello beds which had been extravagantly refurbished for use at La Coste. But he had retained the original mattresses with their impacted springs, so that as a voyeur he could tune his ear to the commentary of lovemaking as it happened in the castle's bedrooms.

At a certain point he decided he had seen enough, and that it was time for him to impose on Marciana in the grandest of the château's bedrooms. At a sign from Donatien, Nina brought him on a chalice the transparent panties that Marciana had been wearing in the theatre. He kissed the item in reverence of his sister, and ran his ring-finger over the shivering fabric. He trembled on contact with the material, and felt his erection type out the secret planetary code that brought him and his sister together. And having offered respect to the most intimate of Marciana's items of clothing Donatien took up a torch and pointed it to the vaulted ceiling. He made a request to Raoul that he should perform the song 'Incestuous Love' on the theatre's mini-stage, so as to additionally ceremonialize the rites in which he would lead his sister out of the theatre and through the corridors lit by cove lights to a scarlet bedroom.

Raoul performed an impromptu acapella version of Barbara's elegiac song in which a parent of forty celebrates the physical love he had shared with a child of twenty. The autumnal feel to the lyrics, and the imagined château in which the song is set, all contributed to the pervading atmospherics at a La Coste furnished for ritual orgy.

Marciana now came to her brother's side, having been especially prepared by Nina, and linked her arm to his, and adopted the conspiratorial sense of *hauteur* that distinguished the Sade family. As Raoul completed the song, so brother and sister left the room to the accompaniment of dark red roses being strewn in their path. Donatien stooped to pick up a rose and place it in his sister's hair. Marciana was wearing eight inch heels so as to accentuate the mould of her bottom as she walked the length of the corridors to the bedroom. Nina was to follow with a camcorder, so that Donatien could re-live the scene on endless repeat. The natural lift and compact curvature to Marciana's bottom, and its elevation on stupendously high heels was of mono-maniacal interest to Donatien. He had resolved never again to miss the chance of augmenting footage of his sister's bottom. The Marquis reflected on how his sister's anus was full of stars, and how he literally fucked the heavens in their sexual discourse. He conceived it that the planets were shot into their respective orbits in Marciana, each time he came. His relationship with his sister had involved the seeding of a new heaven.

The couple walked the length of corridors lined with stuffed animals, and scented with *Eau de Patou*. They were aimed for a bedroom wallpapered with thousands of pairs of Marciana's panties. Donatien had all the time in the world. He had transcended biological decay, and was determined if necessary to exchange his body for a virtual one, should he in time be subject to cellular wear and tear. He would raid XZ's mental database, and extract from the latter's cyberlibrary the information he required to establish a virtual host.

The doors were opened for the couple, before the attendants were free to enter the orgy that had dispersed throughout the château. They were allowed to hear nothing and to know nothing of the sexual rites conducted between brother and sister behind sealed doors at La Coste.

Part V

CYBERLIBRARY

Donatien had planned his meeting with XZ for noon. He had deliberately chosen the library for their agreed rendezvous, as the walls were insulated by the books he had collected over the centuries. Beginning with works of philosophy and mysticism, Donatien had graduated over the years into a bibliophile, and his collection included poetry, fiction, and the new physics, as well as books on astrophysics and pharmaceuticals.

It was in the library he wrote and surfed the Internet for all the accumulating data on cryonics. The furnishings were all in mauve velvet, while the ceiling was painted cobalt as an aid to study and reflection. Donatien kept his black books there, the journals in which he wrote his sexual confessions, and which had accumulated over the centuries to a vast compendium of pathological admissions, all of them leather bound and monogrammed with the Sade crest. *The 120 Days Of Sodom* formed only a small section of a work in continuous progress.

Donatien closed the door of the library and went over to his favourite velvet armchair. He was early for the appointment with XZ, and let his thoughts luxuriate in the idea of his marriage to Marciana on the following day. It would also serve as a marriage of the two châteaux, and excluding the suspect XZ, for whom Donatien felt nothing but disgust, he welcomed the prospect of closer relations between the two sealed castles. He assumed from infonauts on the Internet that other deathless colonies existed on earth, although from much of the data on screen, these appeared to be pockets established by extraterrestrial invasion. Donatien knew that walk-ins were eluding detection, and that a progressive android colonization was taking place in parts of Asia, and on the west coast of America. The Marquis knew that in time he would have to defend his knowledge of DNA and cryonics against the progressive extraterrestrialisation of earth. He suspected that XZ was an infiltrator into both châteaux, and that being in possession of alien intelligence, he was searching for post-biological knowledge in order to assist his cult in establishing supreme rule on earth. Donatien sensed that the man's aspirations were global, and that his impulse-translation of extraterrestrial frequencies gave him an intelligence that could bust the chemical randomness of the human. Space was XZ's modem, and Donatien who belonged to a gothic laboratory intent on inhabiting a present rather than absent body, was concerned that libido should remain an authoritarian part of his species.

XZ entered the library with characteristic cool. To Donatien he resembled a west coast hippie, with his long hair tied back in a pony-tail, and his tight jeans capped by silver knee boots. Donatien knew that XZ had claimed that the destruction of the planet was programmed for 3,083, and that survivors of the catastrophe would be those who had learnt to migrate across the archetypal galaxies of inner space. Donatien felt uncomfortable that XZ should be able to define an exact time for apocalypse, particularly as the supposition was unassailable due to its existing in a hypothetical future.

XZ sat down and crossed his legs, placing one silver boot over the other with meticulous poise. He requested a glass of mineral water, before taking out a dark blue capsule, and unloading the contents of the gelatin shell in water. To Donatien this seemed like a direct act of provocation, but he let the incident go. He was determined to follow no false trail, and had a shadow of suspicion that the capsules were produced for effect, and carried no real significance in terms of affecting biological longevity.

'It's not a matter of challenge,' said XZ disarmingly, suddenly fixing his lenses on Donatien, 'it's more a question of knowing.'

Donatien let the cryptic remark hang haloed in suspense, and realised that territorial prerogative was of no advantage in his relations with a humanoid whose territory was inner space. It was as though XZ had internalised the heavens, and that for Donatien to reach the elusive pinpoint of his personality, he would have to embark on an interplanetary mission.

'We're here,' Donatien proposed 'because we both contain secrets of life-extension. I have little doubt that you are no more willing to part with your formula, than I am with mine. If you have acquired your knowledge through psychic endeavour, then mine is the result of a libidinous humanitarian who has learnt from suffering.'

XZ remained respectfully taciturn, and appeared wholly preoccupied with his own route to the interior. 'There are only two methods of survival that interest me and my cult,' said XZ, 'and one of these is the application of certain meditation techniques to the chakras, and the other is the preparation in time to abandon the body, and to live as an inhabitant of inner space through a virtual body.'

'And pleasure?' questioned the Marquis. 'How will we account for that?'

'Pleasure's conditioned by the quality of lucent inner light,' said XZ. 'The pleasures of out of the body sex are greatly superior to those experienced by physical sex. Astral orgasm is a point of high spiritual attainment. Our cult have developed a sexual vocabulary activated by neural implants which enhance the vibrational frequency of the chakras. Genitals are obsolete. The inner civilizations have outgrown the need for external genitalia.'

'I still maintain a trust in the infinitely reparable body,' said Donatien, feeling his somatic premises threatened by XZ's extrabiological theories. 'We at La Coste have no reason to disinherit the body,' said Donatien. 'Our family is a nuclear libido, it depends on sexual energies for its existence.'

XZ looked away. He appeared neither bored nor disinterested, but simply centred in his own space. Donatien noted that XZ had a guru's coolness, and the sort of non-committal emotions that characterize pilots. He felt more and more certain that XZ was a planetary infiltrator.

'I would place more trust in a tele-existence,' said XZ. 'Why do you assume that physiology should occupy a purely local space? Post-human tele-operators would reach across solar systems, and so defy the concept of being localised by the body. Our cult is about light biology, and the expedients of travel through inner space.'

Donatien saw that he would never extract the motivating dynamic behind XZ's post-human theories. The man's intelligence and his apparent defection from physicality made it difficult for Donatien to confront him on any sympathetically shared plane. Donatien kept imagining that behind XZ's lenses was an implant video display monitor, on which were shown events happening on another star.

'But we can't dispense with biology and remain human,' Donatien asserted, in an attempt to have XZ deliver an identity. 'To my knowledge the immune system is going to wreak havoc on any foreign object you put into the body. Implants will surely be rejected in the process of mutating. And if you suppress the immune system in allowing for the implants, then isn't the body immediately open to viruses and bacteria? The likelihood of infections is going to be astronomical.'

XZ appeared mildly amused at Donatien's pragmatic trust in the body. He seemed to have assessed Donatien's ideas as belonging to another universe, but expressed no display of disdain or scepticism. He looked towards one of the library's high shelves, then moved his eyes back to Donatien, and said, 'you're still constrained by the physical. The experience of my small cult, or rather what happened to us on an isolated Pacific beach, was a transcendence of death without any physical effort. The energies that affected this transcendental state also worked to assist the body in overcoming its biological clock. More than that I can't disclose, and perhaps there are no language equivalents for this sort of experience.'

Donatien was impressed by the gentle tone in which XZ attempted to give an approximate account of his change-over, although he offered no clues as to how this post-evolutionary state was attained. Whatever had happened, he could see, was clearly so much a part of the man that it could never be separated off into language. It remained composite within him.

'I can follow you up to a point,' said Donatien, 'but of course I can't enter into the quality of your experience. Mysticism is a subjective discipline. What you pursue as a cult is individual to your members.'

'But it's also universal,' responded XZ. 'While I'm forbidden to state the exact nature of the experience that transformed both me and my eleven colleagues, we are confident that mankind is evolving towards a similar enlightenment. My work is to help sensitize global vibrations, so that the species as a whole arrive at the place at which I and my cult find ourselves. We can all achieve it – the migration towards hyperspace.'

Donatien realised that he had run into an impasse. To break XZ down would involve enumerating on his own cryonic formulae, by way of setting up a challenge, but he was unwilling to risk the proposition.

'Have you made the Pleasure Château your head-quarters?' he asked.

'It's a necessary modem for the present,' said XZ, 'for there is the beginnings of an alert to the new species. Or at least a sympathy that will accommodate its evolution.'

'And what are your interests in my château?' asked Donatien, in a tone that was uncompromisingly direct. 'I assume you came here out of curiosity.'

'I came to accompany Leanda and Nicole,' replied XZ. 'They are at a formative stage of development, and asked that I should accompany them to La Coste. They have come to acknowledge me as their teacher.'

'La Coste,' said Donatien, with a considerable pride, 'is an ancient establishment, and one in which mystic illumination is attained through extreme sexual practises. Do you not feel threatened here?'

XZ smiled. 'Not in the least,' he said. 'I am always present and absent. To have undergone our particular initiation is to experience many different levels of consciousness at the same time. I'm both here and wherever I choose to be.'

Donatien sensed himself prickling at XZ's elusiveness. He found the man's lack of physical palpability impossible, and so too his evident asexuality. He could find no access to XZ's vulnerabilities, and in this respect regarded him as an alien. He felt estranged from him on every level, but could not help feeling that XZ genuinely carried within him the blueprint to a post-human species.

'I feel La Coste can offer you little,' he found himself saying. 'Tomorrow I shall marry my sister in the chapel, so as to bond our lineage. You will probably disapprove of such a ceremony, and particularly of the incestuous relationship I have been conducting with my sister for centuries. It is through sexual union that I have received the visions that have allowed Marciana and I to live as the deathless ones within the walls of our château. Tomorrow these rites will be consummated by marriage.'

XZ showed no least sign of shock at Donatien's revelations. Instead he sat back deeper in his chair and sipped at a glass of water.

'We all have our own destinies,' he said. 'Mine is to

help others achieve theirs through sensitised inner light. That and no more.'

Donatien allowed himself to enter the erotic reveries attendant on his forthcoming marriage. The most minute particulars of details pertaining to lingerie and dress should be observed, and he would outline his specifications to Nina that night. A pair of panties suitable to the union would have to be selected, so too a gown that would both eroticize and ceremonialize the occasion. Donatien intended the event to be an immemorial extravaganza, and slaves were to work all night in preparing the chapel for the ceremony. He cut himself free of these imaginings, and again made himself present to XZ.

'Will you attend our marriage?' he asked.

'I may be on another frequency at that time,' said XZ. 'I've communications to make with other stations in the galaxy. And there are the disciplines I pursue on a daily level. We meditate and tune ourselves into the universe. As prototypes of the new species we have to work hard at maintaining the right energy levels. I will probably be in meditation at the time of your marriage.'

Donatien avoided being perceptibly ruffled by XZ's imperturbable cool. He was beginning to regret having allowed XZ admission to La Coste, and was determined not to permit him entry to the castle's subterranean mysteries.

'You may not have conceived,' said XZ, 'that you and I are both part of the same genome. That we have split off in very different directions, and yet still come together at a specific point in time, is not without significance. We have something to learn from each other, and I'm confident that we will find a meeting place.'

'I'm not,' said Donatien abruptly. 'If your programme is one of escape velocity, then ours is one of immortalizing the sexual body. These walls at La Coste contain an encyclopedic archive of sexual data. We are rooted in autumn. Our vine is the libido, rich with its pulsing fruit. My family dates back to the tenth century, to Louis de Sade, and is one of the oldest in

Provence and the Comtat Venaissin. It was the child Bénézet who in the year 1177 miraculously lifted a stone so large that thirty men could not have moved it, and set it down on the river's bank where the first arch of a bridge was to be placed. He was instructed to do this by Jesus Christ. This bridge over the Rhône contains the Sade coat of arms on its first arch. I tell you this because of the aspect of building bridges. They demand the sort of foundations that you and I don't share. Their construction is a permanent thing. I believe our interests if they intersect occupy only a transient place in our respective lives. I am rooted in the Sade legend, and my status here is one of miracle.'

XZ continued to remain impervious to any emotive thrust on Donatien's part. 'It's not an issue of lineage or sex,' he maintained. 'As I advise my disciples, there's an occult ganglia to the unconscious. If the ESP sense ducts are opened, then various techniques of lambike yoga can contribute to astral sex. Where I think we differ is over a belief in a future for the body. My cult maintains that only through virtual or absent bodies will there be a future for the species. And that only through migration from the planetary body earth, will we develop as a race.'

Donatien appeared to have closed up. With considerable ostentation he took a bottle of champagne from a freezer next to his desk, tested the temperature with an appraising hand, then detonated the cork. A white plume of smoke escaped the bottle. He took out two glasses from a compartment in his desk, and fizzed a level of wine into each glass. He offered one to XZ, who predictably abstained from the invitation. Donatien lifted up his ticking glass, inhaled the bouquet, and savoured the vivacious fruits of his soil. His recommending smile told everything. He was totally contained by the approving moment. Donatien's sensuality lit his face as he continued to sip at his glass. He was like somebody reading the vocabulary of his vines, and their rootedness in history.

XZ almost took the cue to leave, but remained

unshakeably relaxed in his chair. Donatien could see that the man wasn't going anywhere, and had all the time in the world to be present in his dimension. He continued to place one silver boot over the other, and to stare off into space. Donatien poured himself another glass of champagne, and continued to treat XZ with a degree of aristocratic contempt for outsiders. He was additionally irritated by the knowledge that none of his projected *hauteur* made any least impression on XZ. He decided to bring the meeting to an end, and turned his back on XZ, hoping that the latter would rise and leave. But Donatien was conscious only of the continued silence that described XZ's presence, and of his persistence in staying seated in his chair.

'We don't seem to be communicating,' said XZ. 'I'm somewhere, and you're somewhere else, and while I don't need your space, I feel you have need of knowing about mine. My cult are conditioned to enter a mystico-cyberspace; we're also yogis, adepts at pharmaceutical experimentation, and extraterrestrial surfers. But far more than that, for we will adapt to the future, we are the prototypes of a new race. I'm not saying that your species is obsolete, but that it will be in time, not withstanding your purchase on DNA. It's more a problem of fixity. You're circumscribed by place. No matter how long you live, you're fixed. We're fluent. In a year we will have a keypad that will allow us to communicate directly with a number of near planets. The push buttons will be implanted into the palm of the left hand, and will be digitally operated. In time, spacecraft won't be necessary. We ourselves will negotiate the near planets.'

XZ stopped speaking, and looked away. Donatien watched as he took another blue capsule out of a star-shaped container, and swallowed the pill with water. XZ made no reference to this repeat of his earlier practice, and resumed his usual mode of absolute control.

Donatien returned to his chair and confronted XZ with his usual imperious demeanour. He was not making the least inroad on XZ's defences, and had come to a point where he realised the inefficacy of language to address extraterrestrial issues. Donatien appeared contracted, as though he was settling into deep foundations, and in the process locating a security in his past. He had kept on preparing himself for a mental combat that was indefinitely postponed. He leant forward and took his weight on his elbows. Somewhere underground he could hear his menagerie of castle freaks dragging itself round in heavy chains. He could sense his underworld rising like a black sun in the castle's depths. He struggled with the impulse to go to his own and reclaim his constituency of the captive.

He faced XZ with inflexible scrutiny, and tried for a last time to manoeuvre into a position of superiority. Even in the attempt he could feel his combatant's resistance. Donatien could discover in XZ no interface between human and android. The man was missing the basics of communication, and had withdrawn to a planet in his head.

'I can see we will have to resume our conversation another time,' said Donatien, feeling his expectations zero to the nihil. 'We're finding no common point of agreement. We are both custodians of a knowledge we are unwilling to share.'

XZ continued staring into near or deep space. Donatien had the feeling that he couldn't care less about anything happening in his immediate precinct. He was situated somewhere else.

'If there's nothing my château can offer you by way of sensual pleasures, then I trust you will discover other diversions,' said Donatien by way of a concluding remark.

XZ sat for some moments contemplating his silver boots, then got up, and with no reference to Donatien, made his way out of the door.

Donatien sat a long time staring into abstract space. Every facet of his life jumped into view, and the enormity of the centuries through which he had lived crowded into his consciousness. He saw himself dignified and disgraced, rich and poor, exultant and dejected. He evaluated his place in time and his situation in the body, and trusted in the reality of all that he had known. He was certain that he wasn't living through an illusion, and that the narrative of his days was in its context a preparation for entry into ultimate vision. His marriage to Marciana would affirm that premise.

He thought of Marciana's body and the sacredness he attached to their sexual rites. He told himself that he had found monogamy only through incest, and that the mystic connotations attached to this pact were absolute. Donatien found himself reflecting on the stages of perversion that in turn led to redemption. He thought of how orgasm was a form of somatic ballistics, and that the heightening of it was the equivalent of ecstatic vision. He would sometimes pray on his knees with his cock powerfully fixed in Marciana's bottom. Donation felt that an alteration was occurring in his relationship with time. It wasn't that he felt threatened by mortality, it was more that he was conscious of a fixture existing in his apprehension of time itself. He was experiencing an accelerated movement within himself that thrilled him with a sense of adrenalised expectation. He considered how for centuries he had lived in a non-linear state of suspension, and that he had grown to be completely without anticipation of change. Now he felt as though he had entered into a time stream, and that the feeling had been activated by excitement at his upcoming marriage. Again he could hear the movements of his menagerie in the castle's subterranean interior, and quickly locking the door of his library, Donatien took a lift the twelve flights down to the château's dungeon.

Donatien had mobiled through to the orange-coated Jacques, and the latter was there to receive him at the sealed grid to the underworld. Jacques used a remote to open the grid, and together with Donatien he proceeded through a long cove-lit corridor to a door marked the House of the Six Blondes.

As Donatien entered a scarlet and gilt room designed

to resemble the parlour of a baroque bordello, so six women with extravagantly blonde hair, and all of them dressed in items of leopardskin clothing, got up from their chairs and bowed to the Marquis. Strewn all over the floor were hundreds of lipstick tubes, mascaras, eyeshadows, powder containers, and the whole spectrum of theatrical accoutrements that the girls used as a distraction from unmitigated ennui. They had constantly to make themselves up in case the Marquis should visit without warning, and should their looks appear to him unsatisfactory, then a severe Sadean whipping would ensue. Should the girls satisfy Donatien's criterion, then they would be rewarded by the introduction to their parlour of six sex-starved schoolboys from the local village.

    Donatien commanded the girls to present their bottoms, and he proceeded to check them for beauty spots. He liked at least one pencilled spot to exist in the slit, and preferably on the left hand side of the cheeks. He appeared delighted with his findings, and after scrutinising the minutiae of each girl's bottom, he reminded the girls of their station as sex-slaves. They existed, he said, for no other purpose than to provide pleasure, and the morphology of their buttocks was a commentary on their obedience to rank.

    Donatien took up a number of pencils and sticks of makeup and began applying impromptu *trompe-l'oeil* flourishes to areas of the girls' buttocks. He regarded these six blonde kittenss as a buttocks-harem designed for his personal gratification, or as a diversion to the rampant schoolboys who were sometimes brought in to assuage his harem's frustration.

    Having instructed Jacques to video the proceedings, Donatien went back to the corridor, unlocked a black wooden door, and went inside to find the schoolboys sweating over photographs of their intended conquests. The blondes had been photographed in all manner of com-promising positions, and were dressed in lingerie and stockings. The schoolboys, who were forbidden to wank in the period of waiting, were so excited that they were visibly shaking. Donatien additionally aroused the boys by telling them that the girls were putting on silk stockings to enhance the sensuality of lovemaking. Donatien could see the impacted bulge in each of their jeans, and decided that it was the right moment to supplement their longing with aphrodisiacs. He gave each of the youths a number of sex-sweets, and then fished a little pair of black silk panties out of his pocket. He held the item up and assured them it had been worn by one of the blondes, and that he had just slipped it off her bottom. He went on to tell the libidinous pack that the girls would all be wearing see through panties moist with their urgent need.

When Donatien had aroused the boys to a point of no return, and could see that the aphrodisiacs were kicking into their systems, so he led them out of the room, down the corridor, and told them to wait outside the red and gilt door marked the House of the Six Blondes. Donatien went inside, saw that the girls were arranged in feline postures, concealed himself behind a wall that served as a two way mirror, and then had Jacques open the door with the exaggerated ceremony of a brothel keeper.

The six youths found themselves in an extravagantly baroque interior, with the girls arranged on silk cushions, their legs invitingly arched, and their tongues beckoning through red glossed lips.

The youths uniformly unzipped, struggled out of tight jeans, and with a detonative lust threw themselves on the waiting girls. One volcanic expectation was reciprocated by the other, and in a kicking flurry of long silk-stockinged legs, the blondes snaked their viperine bodies round the hard urgency of the demented youths. Donatien watched as the boys extracted from the blondes an unending series of raucously strangulated cries. It was the meeting of satyriasis and nymphomania. The girls were achieving orgasm with almost every elongated thrust from their desperately urgent partners. They were being pumped to a screaming surrender, and soon the boys were exchanging partners, and were jumping from one rapturously pleasured blonde to the next in a sticky orgiastic maelstrom of bodies.

One boy was wearing a pair of transparent panties over his face, so that he could inhale their perfume while he ferociously fucked their wearer. She could be seen tantalising his balls with long scarlet fingernails, while he worked at her with unabating fury. The scene was exactly as Donatien had anticipated, and was expanding to oral gratification as the groups of bodies grew more complex. It seemed impossible for anyone present to find a liberating form of appeasement, as one orgasm was quickly succeeded by another and another. One of the blondes was being shafted by two youths, and was at the same time rimming a boy who was being orally devoured by a green eyed pussycat. Donatien noted that some of the youths had come six or seven times, but still showed no signs of exhaustion. All of their hothouse fantasies were being fulfilled, and the blondes were in a state of agonized repeat orgasms.

Donatien resisted the idea of thrashing the participants, and settled for the vicarious pleasures of the spectator. One of the youths was being initiated into the cult of the anal staircase, and he buried his penis in the constricted orifice of an insatiable blonde. Donatien observed the boy's ecstasy as he began to rhythmically assert himself and find his way to a different interior.

At the other end of the spectrum, a youth with a wrist-thick erection was being wanked into a pair of transparent panties. The blonde had placed the transparent black fabric over his penis like a face-veil, and the boy rippled with the sensual friction of her wet panties being drawn up and down his indomitable cock. The boy's face commented on the deliciously agonizing pressure that was mounting in his penis. He clearly both wanted to come and didn't, for the pleasure was so overwhelming that he kept holding back on his orgasm. The blonde perfectly under-stood his need, and continued to tickle and tease the nerve-points along his frenulum, withdrawing the panties from contact with his skin each time he was about to explode, and then refitting the fabric to the prepuce and tightening it all the way to the base as the potential orgasm subsided. Donatien envied the youth this protracted form of torment, and decided that at a later date he would have the blonde administer a similar treatment to his sex. The boy was starting to push himself off the ground with his bottom, so urgent was the need to come, and Donatien sensed that he couldn't hold out much longer and would soon surrender to ejaculation. The blonde was tickling him through the invisible black fabric with one red fingernail, and then sensing this time a point of no return, moulded the fabric like a condom to his penis, and sucked him to a tempestuous orgasm. The rush of his explosive semen was delivered in unending spasms, as the blonde positioned herself to take it deep throat.

The other youths were growing progressively more audacious, and three of them were firmly entrenched in their partners' bottoms. They were hard at it in the way that Donatien had spent his life, and he was quick to inwardly commend their movements and experimentation. For a moment he was tempted to join the orgiastics and demonstrate the art of consummate sodomy, but instead he decided to leave his viewing station and visit the Black Room.

The Marquis called for Jacques to accompany him on his journey through a labyrinthine maze of passages that led to the Black Room at La Coste. As they made their way through the corridors, so Donatien would stop at various cages and feed grapes to the occupants. There were midgets in a number of receptacles and a series of snakes and exotic birds. One of the midgets licked Donatien's hand, and received a blessing as a consequence. Donatien fed him large purple grapes, and promised him that in two weeks he would be admitted to the House of the Six Blondes, so that he could appease his sexual frustration.

When Jacques unlocked the three doors to the Black

Room, Donatien took up a position in an anteroom also equipped with two way mirrors and video equipment. What he saw was what he had expected. The room was divided in two by a glass partition, and in one room were an assortment of dusky southern beauties, and in the other a group of tattooed sailors who had been lured to La Coste after docking at the port of Marseilles. Both groups who were regularly fed on aphrodisiacs were prevented reaching each other by the glass partition. The girls sat around in micro skirts and eight inch heels, striking up provocative poses that had the rabid sailors attempting to climb the glass wall, so desperate were they to reach their equally aroused temptresses. Most of the sailors had their cocks in their fists, and the sweat was running in bright drops over their indigo and green tattoos.

    Donatien watched both parties struggle with tormented sexual energies, and after watching the proceedings for ten minutes, he decided he would have the cock-holes opened in the partition. A remote was directed at the screen, and a number of apertures the width of a thick dick appeared in the partition. The sailors all ran towards the glass, and with agonized longing inserted their cocks into the necessary apertures. Their lengths made it through to the other side, and the girls ran forward to begin acts of stormy-haired, frenzied fellatio. Donatien had seldom viewed such voracious appetite for deep-throat. The men were howling with want and fed their cocks into vermilion lips with unsparing ferocity. The girls were all tongue and sibilance as they gorged and choked on rhythmic muscle. Both parties were clawing at the glass, but Donatien was determined that their bodies would never come into contact, other than through the narrow cock-apertures. The sailors were in a state of convulsive orgasm as the girls tongued, kissed and swallowed their pulsating cocks. Strings of incandescent pearls were being ejaculated into throats, and the girls went through motions of nymphomaniacal auto-eroticism as they sucked cock.

    Donatien grew bored with the oral debacle, and

motioned to Jacques to close the apertures. A warning light came on as a sign to the sailors that they should immediately withdraw, and they raged with frustration at being so suddenly separated from their equally frustrated partners. Some of them had been on the point of orgasm, others were in the process of coming, but Donatien's arbitrary decision could never be questioned. The sailors knew that if they protested then they would be whipped near to death by the Marquis De Sade.

Donatien made it clear to Jacques that he would only visit one other room before returning to the château. He had decided on the Mauve Room, and commanded Jacques to lead him still deeper through the tortuous maze of corridors that arteried themselves in the castle's abyssal depths.

Jacques struck out at a fast lick and Donatien followed in his wake. Donatien read the names on doors that he hadn't dared open for centuries, due to the deformities that marked their cowering inhabitants. There was a room marked the Valley of the Freaks, and another one announced the category Two-Headed Hybrids, and still another one Human Bestiary. Donatien lashed each door with his bullwhip, as a reminder that his authoritarian presence had survived the centuries.

The two men continued for a considerable distance, and at last stopped outside a door that was painted purple. As had been his practice in visiting the two previous arenas of sexual perversion, Donatien entered an anteroom, and took up his place seated behind a two way mirror. The room he looked into was the den of the Purple Princess. All the walls were painted purple, and a series of mauve spotlights on dimmers contributed to the almost indigo volume of light that gave the room an underwater density of mauves graduating into blues. The Purple Princess could be viewed sitting in front of a mirror. Her hair was dyed purple, she wore extravagant mauve makeup and a bruise-toned lipstick, and was dressed in a transparent purple nightie shot with gold silk. She had been in mourning for over a century, and Donatien was so moved by her absolute devotion to her dead lover, that he had decreed that no man should ever be allowed to touch her again. Her lover's lips had been preserved, and it was these that she faced, for they had been implanted in the Princess's mirror.

Donatien assured Jacques that if he should die then his sister would observe a correspondingly devotional grief. It brought Donatien incalculable pleasure to imagine Marciana mourning him in a mirrored room at La Coste. Donatien continued to observe the Purple Princess, as she placed an endless series of kisses on her dead lover's lips. She would alternately dab them with light kisses and then crush them with hot-blooded passion. She would place her tongue in her lover's lips like a shrimp attracted to the suction-pad of a sea anemone. Donatien observed her necromantic fixation with a sense of awe. The Purple Princess was the only one of his captives who provoked compassion in Donatien, and he looked upon her as a protector, and as a sympathiser with her extreme grief. He watched her in silence and instructed Jacques to oversee the delivery of a thousand purple and black roses to her room the following day.

Donatien remained watching the Purple Princess for a long time before he decided to leave. He saw this occupation as a necessary shot of emotion to his inflexible psychology. He reminded himself that if in the remote possibility of his ever having to re-encounter reality, then he would need at least a degree of emotional activation if he was to survive.

Donatien opted for a golf-cart as a means of transport back to the château's living quarters. The vehicle hummed through recessed mazes with Donatien occasion-ally stopping to view a particular exhibit in a cage, or to listen to a cacophony of inmates testing their strength against metal doors locked with bolts the width of logs.

When Donatien returned to his quarters, the screams that assailed his ears came from the château's bedrooms. The bedrooms were thumping with excited lovers, and the sound of women's voices imploring their partners to go still deeper and harder raised a throaty chorus of hoarse gratifications to his ears. Somebody nearby was orchestrating a woman to multiple, thrashed out orgasms, and Donatien imagined a man fastened to a she-leopard so intensely animalistic were the extended series of shrieks being extracted from the woman.

Donatien was preoccupied with marriage plans for the following day. Already a vast number of servants were preparing the chapel, and he decided to withdraw to his private rooms and reflect on the monumental idea of marriage to Marciana.

Part VI

NEW DAY

Donatien had decided that his nails should be painted silver with a horizontal orange strip, for his marriage day. Nina sat up with him that night, in one of his familiar night watches at La Coste, and experimented with a variety of makeup colours to suit his pigment, and in the matching of a number of costumes appropriate to the occasion.

Donatien was anxious to extend the night, and to deepen his occupying it by being totally present to the moment. He wanted to situate himself in the great night, and to remember. The payload in his nerves hummed with connections. Donatien was on overload, and his back-tracking through the centuries to isolate memorable particulars lifted into consciousness the good and the ugly. But mostly he celebrated the sexual life he had shared with this sister, the red autumns he had known in his globe-hopping, and finally the joy of resuming life in the permanent autumn that flowered in the microclimate at La Coste.

'The night,' he told Nina, 'is essentially the wolf's hour.' He spoke in terms of it being the flip-side of consciousness, and of how familiarity with the night permitted him to live permanently in the imagination. 'There's no end to the unconscious,' he told Nina, 'a single image is as subdivisively expansive as a black hole. We could journey through imagination for ever in a way that journeyer craft travel out of the solar system into deep space. And the interior of this house is the unconscious,' he observed.

Nina was sitting opposite him, dressed in green silk panties, and mauve velvet thigh boots. She was applying needlework to one of his orange satin shirts, and was re-elasticating the pair of Marilyn's Monroe's black panties that Marciana was to wear on her marriage day.

'Nobody has walked with me at the interior of the castle,' he continued. 'Nobody would dare. The depths of the place are too terrible for even me to penetrate. There are chimeras hidden there, for which no language is adequate. Jacques has come with me into the immediate underworld, but that is an intelligible place in which the sexual freaks can be contained. There is a lift built into a shaft to the depth of five thousand feet. And that is only the beginning of the cages. I have walked there for nights and days and days and nights again, and returned as someone who has undertaken a great journey. I have come back from the interior, and only with Marciana's help have I rehabilitated myself to living in the château.

'I was going to return there tonight, but I have abandoned the idea. I had thought to take XZ there, and to lock him into one of the cells. It may be the only way I will ever extract secrets from him. But instead, I have decided to stay, and to relive memories of my love for Marciana.'

Nina continued sewing. Marilyn's black panties were appropriately translucent and tight fitting. She re-elasticated the band on which they depended, and fastidiously scented them with *1,000*, the complex scent by Jean Patou which was a favourite with Marciana.

Donatien watched Nina's fetishistic handiwork, poured her a glass of pink champagne, and them resumed talking.

'Our marriage, Nina,' said Donatien with enforced gravity, 'is the vision for which all mystics have searched. It will bring about changes in the heavens. Stars will come on, and stars will go out. Our mutual astrobiologies will alter the future of the species.'

Donatien paused for a moment, and looked up at the black velvet ceiling. He was continually amazed that the enormous overreach of his mind could be contained by his body. Despite the input of telemedical repair, he was still composed of cells and genes, and yet for the past hundred years he had not so much as cut himself. Marciana too had enjoyed optimum health, and neither he nor his sister, he reflected, had ever considered the possibilities of illness or disease. He recollected how he had suffered in prison. He had feared the loss of sight, and his body deprived of exercise had grown obese. On reflection, he considered he had suffered enough during the long years of the eighteenth century, and in the years he had spent at Charenton – an institute for the mad.

Donatien could feel the night in his veins. It felt to him like his blood was praying for an extension of dark, and a dawn that when it came would be shot through with stars. He let Nina continue her sewing in silence, for a while, and continued to meditate on the nocturnal aspects of his psyche. He experienced again the indignities and social disgraces he had suffered in a past periodically reduced to the horizons of a freezing cell. For a period of thirty years in his life he had been stripped of freedom. His revenge had been to outlive his enemies and their sons and the sons of their sons. He had lived subsequent to imprisonment, like somebody burning a Cadillac across the American highways. He was determined that no impediment ever again would stand between himself and the open horizon. And now he was resolved that nothing would stand in the way between him and admission to the gates of the mystic city.

He looked across at Nina, and wondered if they would all be altered one day, and correspondingly transfigured by light. He wondered if he would sit with Nina one day in a heavenly mansion, and as he was thinking this, so she arched her legs, and his eye telescoped to the green ridge of fabric tightly encasing her crotch. He traced an orange fingernail over her gusset, and continued to tease it with the distracted air of someone who is evidently bilocated.

'Although I have forbidden it always,' said Donatien, 'I want you to model the black panties that Marciana is to wear tomorrow. I want to see the exact cut on your bottom, Nina.'

Nina stood up, and with a stripper's trained expertise slipped off her green silk panties. Donatien weighed Monroe's black panties in his hand, assessing their transparent flimsiness, and inhaled their scented fabrics. He handed them back to Nina, who slipped them on, and presented her bottom. Donatien's obsessive fascination with the sit of transparent fabric on a heart-shaped bottom was unappeasable. He ran a finger up and down the crack of Nina's buttocks, so as to establish the correct tautness of the fabric. He needed to oversee the exact moulding of the garment to the curvature. There was to be no give to the material, and he was satisfied with Nina's re-elastication of the item. For Donatien a pair of panties had to represent a provocative window on the flesh. He favoured the sort of seamless window in which the garment was indivisible from flesh itself. He had arranged it so that Marciana's trousseau would include a great number of flesh coloured transparent panties, as garments that would prove indivisible on her body.

Nina was asked to model a number of these, with their lace edge in a variety of colours. She was each time asked to present her bottom as evidence of the garment's skintight fit, and correspondingly ordered to submit to Donatien's reinspection of her bottom. After having tried on twenty-five separate pairs of panties, Nina was allowed to return to her sewing.

Donatien returned to his night thoughts. He told Nina of a time in his life when he had visited a Princess's house in the Marais. This woman, he told Nina, liked to have her bottom made up like a cake. She would lie face down on the bed, her midriff supported by cushions, 'and it was my job,' said Donatien, 'to place the hundreds of edible pearls in the glazed icing sugar that coated her buttocks. I had the decorations look like constellations on her ass. The more pearls I placed on her bottom, the more there were to lick off. When the pearls had set on the icing sugar, the masked Princess would open the red velvet curtains and go and stand in the window with her bottom facing the street. And when she tired of her exhibitionism she would draw the curtains again, and ask me to extract the cake decorations from her bottom with my teeth. I omitted to say that the crack of her bottom was filled in with icing sugar too, and it was to this chasm that I was to hungrily return. She would call that place the wedge or the ravine, and it was so sensitive an erogenous site that my oral contact with it would be sufficient to give the Princess multiple orgasms.

'My reward was money, and hers pleasure. I had to count the pearls as I extracted them from their setting, and it was the process of numbering them out loud that added to her excitement. She would grow progressively more stimulated as the numbers increased. It was to my advantage to have sprinkled hundreds of pearls on the icing sugar, and I on completing their extraction was then rewarded with the right to sodomize her. The Princess was exceptionally beautiful, and her bottom suitably matched my fantasies. The silk bed on which I would fuck her would look like a detonated patisserie by the time the ritual was completed. It's something, Nina, that I had never done before, and have never participated in since. That a woman could derive her sole sexual pleasure from this game is amazing, but the ritual was rendered more bizarre by the fact that I had to telephone her husband, and while she listened, describe what had occurred in the minutest detail. The Prince would invariably ask the same obsessive questions with the urgency of a man who is both turned on by phone sex, and repelled by his own insatiable curiosity to learn of his wife's infidelities. The nature of these telephone conversations never changed in the two years of my being paid to make them. While I spoke to the Prince, his wife would sit on my lap in crotchless panties and gently make love to me. The Prince's fascination, expressed always in exactly the same phraseology, was with how many pearls had been lifted from his wife's bottom, how long to the precise second had it taken me to extract the entire constellation of pearls, and what colour panties his wife was wearing at this particular moment.

'He appeared interested in no other topic, and no attempt on my part was made to engage him in any different form of conversation. His manner was totally matter of fact, and his cordially expressed gratitude for the details given him seemed without any conscious affectation. I would leave the Princess's apartment with a cheque that included two signatures, and would be told to return the following week. It was a procedure that went on for several years, until such time as she divorced, and her second husband put a stop to the extravaganza.'

Nina looked up from her sewing, and Donatien who had stopped talking, went over and stood by the heavily curtained window. He appeared to have surprised himself with his memories, and sat down and poured himself a glass of wine.

'The marriage will take place at noon,' he informed Nina. 'I want you to spend the morning preparing my sister's bottom with massage and oils. I want her cheeks to be at their finest. Poems and prayers will be read in the chapel throughout the morning. We are to have ten thousand dark red roses to celebrate the occasion. The marriage bed should be enhanced by perfumes, and Marciana is to wear the 2-denier silk stockings that are especially made for her in Paris. See that she wears black lipstick and that her face is made up like a doll's. I want a single heart-shaped ivy leaf picked from the château's walls, to be placed in her hair. And I wish in the unlikelihood of death occurring to either or both of us in the next thousand years, to have Marciana similarly dressed for her coffin. We are to be joined for ever. Marciana's black wedding panties are to be in your care as from the day following the bridal night. They will be framed and displayed above the altar in the chapel.

'And I have another request. That the Purple Princess, who lives in the château's subterranean vaults, should attend the marriage and be given a place of honour in the ceremony. This woman has never ceased to move my heart, by her unsparing devotion to her dead lover's preserved lips, and to his memory. She is to be escorted to the chapel, and if necessary the mirror in which her dead lover's lips are preserved, should accompany her to the ceremony. See that she is dressed in her familiar purple, and give her whatever comfort and consolation is necessary to her continuing grief.'

Donatien returned to his brooding nocturnal memories. He knew that his earthly marriage would be celebrated in heaven, for he and his sister were already living as the deathless ones. He anticipated Laura's etheric body being present in the chapel, her impulses transmitting visionary light to the occasion. Laura would be Lady in White, his tutelary guardian over the centuries.

Donatien again consciously filled the night. He was present to each moment in its totality. He could feel his nervous system extend like a neural tree across the heavens. His heartbeat was like a cursor making tracks in the stars. He could sense his body make its tele-extension throughout the galaxy. The night had always been his refuge. He had conducted his dionysian rites in the night; he had taken refuge in its conspiratorial dark as an escaped prisoner hunted across the face of Europe. Donatien felt he had always been married to the night. He had lived in its intimate and protective secrecy. He had, he reflected, watched angels walk down deserted roads at night. He remembered the blonde girl he had discovered sitting on the roof of her Citroen in the middle of a field, her body naked, her face and arms lifted to the stars. Donatien was frightened to alert too many associations. Over the centuries he had accumulated so many memories, and the accessing of these could be like confronting a blizzard without protective clothing. He slipped in and out of the past, alternately troubled and elated by his findings. He imagined himself in another thousand years, and tried to envisage how he would ever retain the memories that spanned the epoch. This, Donatien reflected, was his only anxiety in connection with indefinitely sustained longevity. He wondered if he would ever be capable of sustaining the memories. And then he contemplated his marriage, and knew in that moment the journey had been worthwhile. Marciana's hand was to his mind the equivalent of a star, and her anal passage was the entry to an internalised gold palace.

Outside he could hear the continuous rain. It streamed into his recognition as counterpointed dialogue. He could hear it washing through the dense oaks, and enveloping the surrounding countryside in a dazzling haze. He wanted it to rain all night and all day and night. He had the idea that the château was an island, and that rain was blowing in from a grey marbled sea. He imagined there were wrecks in the garden, and that liners had foundered in their passage round the coast.

He would stay up all night, and savour the intensity of each moment. He know that Jacques would be urgent to fuck Nina, and he accompanied her to the bedroom where her urgent lover was waiting. He told her that she was allowed only twenty minutes with Jacques, on this momentous night, when he so needed her attention, and Donatien decided to wait outside the bedroom door for the allocated period of time.

Nina disappeared into the bedroom wearing nothing but flesh coloured panties, and an equally transparent bra. Donatien could hear Jacques imploring her favours. The latter must have immediately placed her over his knee, for he could hear the sound of Nina's bottom being alacritously spanked. It was a register that never ceased to thrill Donatien. He knew from the sound that Jacques was spanking Nina through the skintight nylon that windowed her bottom, while Jacques' intermittent gasps suggested that they had repositioned themselves for a backward 69 interlude, and Donatien could hear the sounds of Nina engorging her lover's strainingly taut muscle. Nina must have impressed on Jacques that they were allowed only twenty minutes, for Jacques sounded desperate in his urgency to come. This was achieved with agonisingly convulsive sounds, and still unappeased, Donatien could hear Jacques flip Nina onto her back and enter her with direct authority. The noise of their intense fucking was one that had the bed smack violently against the walls. It sounded to Donatien as if the bed was walking around the room, as Jacques thrust harder and harder into the compliant Nina. When the bed began to stampede, Donatien knew that the couple were near to coming. Nina's shriek was extended again and again as Jacques buried his urgency in her interior.

Donatien decided to walk back down the corridor and wait for Nina in his room. He know that the hours ahead were to be occupied with nothing but the thought of his marriage. He could smell the night as it lived in the castle's deep corridors. The night to him was also the scent of Marciana's skin, and he found it under her tongue, under her arms, and in all the secret crevices of her erogenous zones.

Nina returned to his room with her hair and face flustered from her recent exertions. Her eyes were lit with intense passion, and the bruised lipstick describing her mouth looked like a number of crushed raspberries. The stimulated pheromones had vitalised her skin, and Donatien could imagine the inflammation of her sensitive vulva.

Donatien continued to drink and reminisce. He had decided to sanctify his marriage through the letting go of redundant memories. There was much to keep, and much to exorcise. He intended the marriage to sanctify the best of him, in a way that would allow him to make a direct pact with the angelic realms. And only then would he have secured his objectives.

Nina, who had checked progress on the wedding preparations informed Donatien that the chapel had been made ready, and that a heart-shaped space described by red sequins had been prepared as a performance area for Raoul. The chapel had been draped in red and black and purple, and girls dressed in angelic costumes were to stand on various elevations during the ceremony, and to shower the assembled guests with bleeding-heart roses.

Donatien began feeding himself the aphrodisiac tinctures that accounted for his indomitable phallic mastery of his sister. He intended to give himself an erection that would last for twenty-four hours. In this time, he estimated, he would introduce Marciana to paradise.

Donatien reminded Nina that six boys with their naked bottoms sprayed purple were to bend over as a salute as he entered the chapel. Their genitalia he insisted were to be glittered with silver, and their hair glammed with frosted gel.

Donatien continued to drink a vintage fermented from the château's vineyards. The wine was his life force, and its colour that of undying autumn.

Nina was now through with her last revisions to the refortification of Marilyn's black panties, and assured Donatien that after Marciana had worn them, they would become one of the sacred heirlooms at La Coste.

Donatien briefly resumed his night thoughts, imparting to Nina now and then some recollection retrieved from the crowded events of his stormily unpredictable life. He remembered being driven in a Rolls across America, the car heading from the East to the West coast pursued by *mafiosi*. Donatien told Nina of how he had been conducting magic sex rites in the desert, and had been hunted across the States by members of an opposing lodge. Donatien told Nina how he adopted drag in order to elude his opponents, and of how he had worn constrictively tight skirts and satin pumps for weeks on end, until he had finally thrown his assassins off the trail.

Donatien fished for selective memories. He could sense the passage of time, and the glow in his abdomen informed him of the repressed excitement he felt at the prospects of marriage. He looked around him at the furniture which had survived the château's original ransacking in the French Revolution, and took in the books, the lacquered chests, the blue tapestries, the Chinese jars, the original flyers for various of his plays, and the general ephemera on show which contributed to his sense of continuity. He wondered why after so many centuries, he wasn't tired, and why he and his sister had been elected as the prototypes of a new species.

He informed Nina that before settling to his prayers and preparations for the coming service, he would like a bottom parade. She was to select from the castle's harem a number of boys and girls who were to visit Donatien at dawn. Donatien had decided that this viewing would distract him from the possibilities of feeling too isolated or too dehumanised in the long night watches. He was secretly frightened of remembering too much. For some reason he had found himself situated in 1790, at the time of his separation from his wife, and the beginnings of a new affair with Marie Quesnet. They had set up house in two properties on the rue de la Ferme des Mathurins, in Paris, and much of the furniture now on display before his eyes had been transposed to those two houses. He recollected the stimulus of that new beginning in 1790, and juxtaposed it with his intention of marrying his sister. If the one had represented the coming together of two people in difficult historic times, then the other represented the timeless incestuous consummation to which he had always aspired.

When Nina returned she was accompanied by six of the château's best bottoms. Both sexes were wearing face veils and rhinestoned G-strings, and Donatien who took up a seat central to the room ordered that the seraglio should walk around him in a continuous circle for fifteen minutes. In this way his trained eye could appraise proportions of the blindside face which fascinated him to a degree of madness. But Donatien could find nothing exceptional in the molecular composition of the three male and female bottoms on display. They were heart-shaped, nut-shaped and epsilon-shaped, but lacked the square within the circle that so distinguished Marciana's buttocks.

Donatien had decided not to fuck any of the bottoms on show, but to devise a game of hunt the instruction. The three girls and three boys were duly blindfolded, and then bent over a sofa. Donatien took a lipstick, and with its red point wrote a series of erotic imperatives on each of the twelve cheeks. The rules of the game were that each person should then form a chain, and act on whatever were the instructions written on the bottom in front of them.

The six individuals were placed in a line, and their blindfolds were removed. They had no option but to obey whatever confronted them, for the failure to do so would result in a severe thrashing from Donatien. It was Donatien's way of choreographing an opportune orgy. He advised the company that they had only fifteen minutes at their disposal to live out their fantasies, and then retired to his chair to observe the proceedings. The way in which the pairing fell was random, and in one case two girls faced each other, and the order comprised boy, girl, girl, boy, girl, boy. Dildos were made available to the girls, for one girl had been commanded to sodomize the other, while it was intended that the third girl in the party should sodomize the boy. This weirdly contrived geometry afforded Donatien a sense of perverse pleasure, as he watched the often mismatched couples attempt to conjugate bodies. At the end of the proposed fifteen minutes he brought the orgy to a peremptory termination with a single whip crack across the wall. The incongruously coupled partners dropped down from exhaustion, before being revived again with copious amounts of champagne.

It was to be Donatien's last distraction before the great ceremony in the morning. He dismissed the orgiasts as though they were inconsequential ephemera, and changing his jacket to black in accordance with his night thoughts, he again took up with his inner dialogue.

At some stage in Donatien's introspective drift, Nina

must have gone over to the window and reported on the change in the autumn sky. She told Donatien that the morning star had never shone brighter, and that the night was receding. The light in the sky, she said, belonged to his marriage day.

Donatien composed himself for the monumental hours to come. He intended the marriage to carry an extravagance paralleled by nothing in the history of his ancient family. The marriage bed on which he was to sodomize Marciana would comprise the compounded heads of five thousand red roses. On that floral platform he would be initiated into angelic secrets. Marciana's bottom as he knew it, was a receptacle for the galaxies.

'The world will change as a consequence of this marriage,' Donatien said out loud to Nina. 'We will never be the same again. We will all begin the process of divinisation. And not as XZ has experienced it, but as a gradual awareness of a journey begun.

'Security is to see to it that XZ does not attend the service,' Donatien added. 'I will not have a walk-in present,' he asserted. 'The man is a virtual intruder, and his alien intelligence is not welcome here. Our coding of cryogenic knowledge is not something I will have him infiltrate. At the same time he's too valuable for me to eliminate. I could have him taken to the château's subterranean cages, but that would turn his cult against us. La Coste would have to withstand avenging extraterrestrials.'

Donatien resumed pacing across the purple carpet. His restlessness showed in the way he appeared to be listening to some internal prompting, as though a voice was speaking from his interior. He crossed and re-crossed the purple carpeted arena, his mind dilated with astral theorems, and appeared to be pondering the greatness of the coming day. It seemed to him that he had come this far against all possibilities. He had arrived, and should go on arriving, he told himself, and there was great courage needed to individuate according to his incarnation.

Donatien found himself fearing revolt from within the château. He had so often listened at night to the dull underground roar emanating from the castle's labyrinthine abyss. Some of these captives he reflected, had been imprisoned in the vaults for three centuries, and he was unable to countenance the prospect of facing their age or probable metamorphoses. He knew that he could never risk penetrating the château's depths. To do so, he imagined, would be like stepping direct into the worst recesses of his unconscious. It was an insoluble and recurring problem for him, his inability to silence the inmates. He checked again with Nina that the Purple Princess had been notified of the marriage, and asked that she should be brought to him for a brief conversation. Donatien knew that this would help to warm his emotions, in the way a singer warms his voice, and certain that all the preparations had been undertaken to ensure the extravaganza of the chapel's interior, he settled himself and waited for the Purple Princess's arrival.

Donatien swung round in his chair, and the heartbroken Purple Princess was quite suddenly standing in the room. She still held the mirror in which her dead lover's lips were mounted, and tears had smudged her mascara. Her body showed nude through her shot silk negligée. This woman seemed no longer to care about herself in any way, and Donatien was able to enter direct to her centre. The Purple Princess allowed him to conceive of what it would be like to be a woman. In his imagination Donatien was himself as a lachrymose diva, all piled up hair and panda eyes and seam-splitting sheaths.

The Purple Princess was shown into a chair by Nina, and there she sat facing the mirror from which she could never be separated. Her black lipstick defined an unsmudgable gloss, and before she would even look at Donatien she bent forward and worked her lips into her dead lover's.

Donatien let his head rest on his hand, and experienced a state of deep empathy with the disconsolate woman who refused to enter into any other relationship than that of mourning for her deceased love. He looked at her distraught vulnerability, and was moved by the irrevocability of her uncensored grief. He would like to have been able to step inside her, and reverse her loss. He had decided a long time ago that whatever the circumstances of his life, there would be room in it for the Purple Princess.

Donatien was attentive to her every need, and he couldn't help but think how her dead lover's body must have fitted her generous curves. Her nipples were splashed with areolas the colour of black pansies. Her bottom was moulded to invite desire and her lips professed the full sensuality of a flower split open by loaded stamen. The Purple Princess emanated a mystique and untouchable provocation that Donatien savoured in a corresponding manner to the admiration he nurtured for his sister's monogamous dignity.

Donatien asked about her life, intending by his enquiry to relate to her feelings of loss, rather than to her everyday living. 'I know there can be no end to your suffering', he said, 'but is there no way in which we can resituate or revision your grief? I'm thinking that with our discoveries at the château, we will soon be able to access the dead through virtual travel. As death is about entering another space, then in time we will take you there.'

Donatien could sense that the strategy he had adopted was making no inroads on the Purple Princess. She continued to consult the mirror with obsessive regularity. Donatien had observed that it was impossible to break the circuit of her grief. If a gap showed in the Princess's eyes, then it was like an internal speck in her eye that would never clear. And he guessed that without the irritant, the Purple Princess wouldn't know how to function.

She sat opposite him, crossing and uncrossing her catwalk legs. Donatien had the idea that if it wasn't Marciana who he was to marry, then it would be the Purple Princess to whom he would devote his life.

Donatien felt inadequate to his task of alleviating the Purple Princess's grief. He left her settle to her resting point, which was a state of introspective distraction. But he was gratified to see on looking up once that she smiled in his direction. It was a smile that appeared to have been years in the formation, as though it had been lifted from an impossible interior. When he looked again, it had gone, and Donatien found himself constructing the metaphor of desert rain to the dust-choked cactus.

Donatien spoke of his imminent marriage to his sister. He told the Purple Princess of the profound significance this union constituted, and of how he surmised that she alone would understand the spiritual overview of the undertaking. There was a tragedy implied by such a union, he added, and one almost comparable to the original fall. Donatien explained to the Princess that should his mission be denied by the angels, then his own fall would be irredeemable. He risked, he said, having his name erased from the Book of Life by taking his incestuous marriage to heaven. He told the Purple Princess that even though the idea was sanctioned by his tutelary guardian, Laura, and that she had appeared in vision to him throughout the marriage preparations, he was still apprehensive that he would offend the spiritual orders.

Donatien poured another drink and settled deep in his chair. He was beginning to feel time as a speeded up phenomenon, as though the illusory suspense created by the night's deep watches had been converted into a more rapidly relayed transmission of events. He knew instinctively that the dawn had arrived in the permanent autumn that existed at La Coste. The happening was coded in his nerves.

To his amazement Donatien noticed that the Purple Princess was sitting with a melancholy smile framing her downturned lips. He could sense a give in her emotions, as though a contracted coil had ever so slightly expanded. It wasn't much, but it looked to him like a beginning.

Nina came into the room and advised the Marquis that

it was time for him to start the elaborate ritual of dressing. He insisted that the Purple Princess stay, and Nina began shaping his eyebrows. Nina wanted to exaggerate the wide space beneath the brow, so she plucked stray eyebrow hairs, and recreated the arc with a pencil. She wished to create a 1930s feel with Donatien's eyeshadow, and to this affect she introduced pure gold to his lids, and then added a mauve sheen. She mascaraed his eyelashes, and added a transparent foundation. He had chosen to dress in purple and black; their sombre, but majestical tones evoking his authoritarian role as a watcher over the centuries. Donatien was to wear a purple satin shirt and a Regency styled black velvet coat. His black velvet trousers were fitted into black knee boots.

As he dressed with Nina's assistance, he remembered the happy days in the mid-eighteenth century, when he would return to La Coste after a journey to Avignon. He recalled how he would take the Apt road, and he would then turn right at Notre Dame de Lumières, or else he would proceed as far as the Julien Bridge and cross the Calavon, from where he would look across at farms lying in the shadow of the blue Luberon mountains. He saw himself again on a sinuous path bordered by the gothic arch of the Clastres gate, and on to the castle ramparts. At that time his true destiny had been only germinating, although he realised that he had always lived at an angle to society, from his earliest days. He threw his mind back to the Chinese pines, cedar, and stone quarries that had surrounded the estate. They had resembled empty film sets, and he could smell the fragrance of lavender rising off the back of a field on a day so long ago that it seemed impossible he was still alive. On that summer's day bees had stumbled as topheavy satellites through the loaded grasses. He remembered how the sunlight had bleached everything to his foreground, and how he had believed that time had stopped suddenly in the mountains. He had been isolated in time as though a photographer's flash had frozen him in the instant.

Nina left Donatien alone with the Purple Princess and

went off to add the final touches to Marciana's dress. The chapel had been prepared by the castle's staff with an even more extravagant panache than had gone into choreographing the chapel for Raoul's concert. The red, black and purple drapes were all monogrammed with the arms of Sade: a star with eight golden rays on a field of gules. The abundance of dark red roses in the chapel bled into presence as a romantic backdrop. Nina had told Donatien that the air was so loaded that making contact with it was like dropping a live microphone. There was to be no officiator over the marriage, and Donatien had decided that he and Marciana would be bonded by each placing a ring on the other's finger. There was to be a castrati choir, and Raoul was to ceremonialise the occasion by singing Barbara's 'Incestuous Love.'

Donatien crossed the room and placed his hand in the Purple Princess's. He knew from her warmth that a tacit bond of love would exist forever between them. His wound corresponded to her own, and his unbearable scar in being excluded from reality, was matched by the inseparable gulf placed between her and her dead lover.

There wasn't much time to wait. The arrangement was that Marciana would be led to the altar wearing a black sheath, and her hair bunched with roses and ivy picked from the château's walls. He answered his mobile once, and was assured that XZ had elected to stay in his room and meditate. Leanda and Nicole, each dressed in transparent negligées would escort Marciana to the altar. Nina had arranged for the altar vessels to be filled with gold sequins. The entire party were to be blessed with sequins. It was all only minutes away.

It had taken him three and a half centuries to reach this threshold. He offered the Purple Princess his arm. It was another beginning to his continuity. He could hear the rain slamming down outside as an accompaniment to his assault on heaven.

Appendix

MORE TALES OF THE MIDGET

Alice Through The Looking Glass

Alice lived in the restored wing of an otherwise vacated gothic mansion on the edge of the city. She arched her legs in the voluminous marble bath, pushed them up vertical, as though they were being appraised by the posters of Elvis Presley and the Marquis De Sade on the opposite wall, and then with her head supported on the rim, kicked them back over her shoulders. She liked to tickle herself in this posture, her pussy dripping with scented foam, and to imagine a spectator observing her through the two-way mirror her uncle had ingeniously contrived to incorporate into the bathroom restoration. Alice fantasised that she was being watched. The spectator would be cupping his balls with his left hand, and working on his cock with the right. He would modulate his virtuoso rhythm, anxious to restrain his crisis until the exact moment when Alice cried out from her solitary pleasure. And her red fingernails worked slowly, expertly over her shaved pussy, the little jewel that she depilated with such extreme attention to detail. She dipped her forefinger in and wriggled. If only Presley, in his tight hipsters would step down off the wall, unzip and mount her without a word of introduction, or De Sade would come out of his formal 18th century pose, and brandish a cane across her soft, nubile buttocks.

Alice had just turned her eighteenth birthday, but she looked considerably younger, and liked to put her hair in ribboned plaits, and to wear a pleated micro-skirt which emphasised her long, curvy legs. Her uncle called her his divine cock-teaser, and Alice never objected to his following her up the tall staircase, he staying back a number of stairs the better to see all the way up her disarmingly short skirt. She got moist from that little game, and several times on his return from lengthy stays abroad, she had opportunely walked out of the bedroom in her black bra and panties to find him stationed in the corridor as though already anticipating her flouncily provocative streak to the bathroom. Was someone outside now? she asked herself, as she began to quicken the rhythm of her fingers, her voice starting to rise as she felt her pleasure increasing. It was excruciating. She ached with the fantasy of having a thick cock pushed into her now, right on the edge of orgasm. Or even better, two. She would gag on the smooth columnar one, while a knottier heavy weapon pinned her with its remorselessly vigorous thrusts.

Alice heard her voice throatily scream with pleasure. She had forgotten, or half forgotten, that her uncle's parasitical valet, Frank, was still in, and probably lying on his bed flicking through the girlie magazines he collected from the fifties and sixties. Alice had discovered boxes of vintage *Playboy* and pin-up magazines in Frank's wardrobe. More discreetly posed than today's nudes, Frank was clearly obsessed by the variety of stocking shots available to the reader, most of the models emphasising the seductive appeal of seamed stockings and suspenders. Alice wondered about Frank. She knew of his preference for wearing false eyelashes, and she had been tempted to leave a pair of her used black knickers on his pillow to see the response this action would provoke. Frank must have been a youthful forty, and it had been his job to drive her
to and from school in her uncle's Bentley, and it was then she had acquired the provocative backseat poses of a teenage tart. Defying school regulations by wearing white see-through panties under her gymslip, Alice had sat reading in the rear of the car, her legs arched in a way that allowed Frank to see everything in the driving mirror. On the road home she would

apply eye make-up, and with her legs angled over the empty front passenger seat, and her hem retreating to the area of her hips, she would read Sade's *Justine* as the car hummed through the lanes leading to their gothic retreat.

Alice sank back into the bath in the afterglow of her sustained pleasure. It had never occurred to her that Frank might be intimate with her uncle's system of two-way mirrors, and that he could at this very moment be observing her masturbatory ritual in the bath. The thought far from repulsing her, had her tingle with pleasure. She would make her emergence from the bath, and the subsequent process of getting dressed, a protracted and tantalising one.

Alice stepped out of the bath nurturing the pretence that Frank was watching her, and began teasingly to dry herself with a towel, presenting her round pink bottom to the voyeur's eye as she bent down in pursuit of an imaginary hairpin. He would see right up her crack. She was saving her little trick of pencilling a beauty spot on her right buttock until later. If Frank was out there wanking, he would shoot up his nostrils at the sight of that precocious ornamentation of her bum. Alice busied herself in the mirror, plucking an eyebrow into a pencilled arch, and spending a lot of time studying her sensitively refined features. She placed two violet ribbons in her plaits to accentuate her schoolgirlishness, and then applied a sensuous oil to her thighs, her shaved pubic triangle, and more leisurely and demonstratively into her glowing buttocks. If Frank was watching, his cock would be in his fist, stiff as a policeman's baton. Alice then proceeded to dress with a pashir's enticement. She snapped on a black translucent bra, and then worked her black see-through panties up from the ankles to the backs of her legs, all the way up until the transparent fabric was filmed tightly against her bottom. She patted her cheeks saucily, and ran a fingernail down the length of her crack. She then fastened her black suspender belt around her waist, dabbed perfume behind her knees, put on her lipstick as a vivaciously flirtatious insignia, buttoned up a red silk blouse, put on a tiny pleated mini, and decided to leave the rolling on of her stockings until later. Already, she felt like fingering herself again. The process of dressing up always had her moist. Alice was perpetually slippery at the crotch. Deciding to pursue her fantastic game to the end, she sat back in the bathroom chair and elongated then bent her leg to the knee as she slipped on a seamed stocking, manoeuvring it from the knee up, until the black stocking top was secured by the suspender fastening. She sat with one leg down and one arched, and then repeated the process on the left leg, and stood up to check the aligned verticality of her seams. If Frank was watching he would have fisted his semen into an ejaculatory plume by now, a hot ribbon of percolated lust. Alice delayed a moment, then slipped out into the corridor, and as she did she was certain she heard a bedroom door close. Frank must have slipped back to his lair, either inflamed or appeased by what he had seen.

Alice was in the mood to tart it up, she was simmeringly restless, and slipping on her spike heels she rapped past Frank's door with an exaggerated staccato click to her heels. She felt the impulse to run her heels abradingly down his spine and knead them into his taut buttocks. Instead, she went to her rooms, and slammed the door. Another Presley poster was looking down at her from above the bed, and she flicked a finger over his crotch, then insolently stuck out her tongue at the immortalized star. She collapsed on her bed and thought of Steve, the schoolboy whose virginity she had taken by blowing him on his mother's bed. She had tormented him by refusing access to her pussy, and then shocked him by an oral expertise that had him convulsing in paroxysmic ecstasy on his mother's silk counterpane. And after deep-throating him to near orgasm, she had disengaged his penis at the moment of climax and his come had shot all over the counterpane. And leaving him no time in which to recover from the confusion of the situation, she had abruptly exited from the room, and had never dated him again. Alice was living out her uncle's epithet of being a divine cock-teaser.

Bored by her life of idleness and luxury, Alice was in search of sensation. Her uncle wasn't due back from South America for another week, so she lacked a dinner companion and someone whose conversation about the bizarre, the weird and the wonderful, helped assuage the feverish excitement with which she anticipated a hedonistic future. Several times she had sat at the table fingering herself while her uncle alluded to encounters in the red light districts of innumerable capitals. On another occasion she had come to the table wearing crotchless knickers under her skirt, so that her furtive access to vicarious pleasure should go unimpeded. Pussy juice had trickled sweetly down her thighs with the scent of guava.

Alice itched in her see-through panties. She spread her legs and fantasised. She wondered how Frank would take her, would he put her up on her haunches, or would he command her on top with his omnipotent possession of her body? And anyhow, she would enact her plan. She listened attentively to hear when Frank would leave his room, and at an opportune moment when he slipped out to the bathroom, Alice sped into his room with a pair of unwashed black silk knickers she had fished out of the washing bag, and placed the choice item on Frank's pillow, in a way that would have him instantly recognize the wearer. The dankly perfumed fetish was a knicker-collector's paradise, and Alice imagined Frank fitting the intimately scented silk to his vibrant erection. She sucked her thumb in anticipation, and curled up on the bed in a Lolita pose, tracing a finger over her lower left buttock, and extending it to that whole erogenous zone. Alice wished she could elongate her neck sufficiently to lick her own pussy, and to lap at her fidgety clit.

She heard Frank return to his room, and the door clicked shut. Silence washed over the house again like a lake rising on itself. Alice scratched at her knickers a couple of times and waited. There was no way in which Frank could ignore a black triangle draped over his pillow. Panties were recognisable anywhere, even if you encountered them in the most unlikely place, like dropped out of somebody's launderette bag onto the pavement, or accidentally pulled out of a jacket pocket when searching for a pen. Alice waited. She was so wet she sat in a slick of juices, but she refrained from rubbing herself in the hope that Frank would come to her room.

She put on her headphones and listened to an old Donna Summer CD, before growing suddenly aware there was a knock at the door. Alice had deliberately laddered her stockings in order to heighten her tartiness, and she strutted over to the door and opened it so that she was concealed to the caller. She waited, and Frank walked tentatively into the room. He was dressed in nothing but her tiny black knickers, his cock straining over the elasticated band, and he had brushed his false eyelashes with mascara. He looked like a transvestite slut, and it was clear to Alice that he had come to teach her a lesson. Frank had never to her eyes looked so sexually assertive.

Alice shut the door and followed him into her room. She wolf-whistled at the wiggle of Frank's ass, her black bikini knickers cutting into his white flesh. The conspiratorial atmospherics in the room were like the preconditioned culmination to a rite which both had been planning for years. 'You want to be fucked, you little hooligan,' Frank said, and it was the first time Alice had ever heard him speak out of character, 'Your knickers will soon be soggy when I stretch your cunt. Don't think I haven't seen you dressing and undressing in the bathroom, scratching your twat, and pencilling beauty spots on your bum. Alice through the looking glass, that should be your cock-teasing name.'

Alice loved hearing Frank talk dirty, and she rolled compliantly on the bed, and began to tease him by running a red fingernail over the crotch of her see-through panties.

Frank flipped her over, and roundly spanked her wriggling schoolgirl bottom until it glowed. 'Not so simple,' he said. 'Go into the bathroom, and sit in the chair and finger yourself, and I'll watch in the mirror.' Alice duly complied, spreading her legs and working herself to feverish orgasm, her voice crying out with frustration and pleasure.

'Come out, you little tart,' Frank dictated, and Alice pushed her skirt down, clicked to attention with her heels, and scurried back into the corridor. She looked all in a flutter, and with her hair in mauve ribbons, she resembled an excited schoolgirl. 'Into my room,' Frank demanded, and Alice entered Frank's strictly male domain, which except for a few bottles of spirits and what Alice recognised as a generous sprinkling of her stolen knickers strewn like trophies across the bed, was an uncluttered, masculine space. There was a scent of cologne in the room, and *Playboy* magazines ware stacked in archival boxes. Alice sensed a conspiratorial link between Frank and her uncle, in fact she half expected her uncle to appear at any moment in one of his elegant silk kimonos, his cock projecting horizontally from a fold in the silk. The result would no doubt have been a long complicated fuck extending three ways until dawn.

'Lick me, you teenage cocksucker,' Frank commanded. 'Get down on your knees and shampoo my dick, bitch.' Alice was greedy to obey, and she slid to her knees and began licking the cock she had disengaged from her own black knickers. She tongued him from the base of his scrotum to the tip of his cock. She wolfed him down with hot rapacity, a salacious smile consuming her features. She worked on him with a consummate knowledge gained from sampling schoolboy's cocks on so many backseats of cars, and from assimilating any number of erotic videos. There was no limit to the culinary art of giving head.

Frank backed off from her gorging lips. He wanted to prolong the pleasure of seeing Alice on heat. He would like to have sat under a glass table and observed the whole geometry of her pudenda from that level, the depilated lips spread open for his enquiry, the shaved crack terminating in her tight anal bud.

Alice awaited her next command. She went down on her knees with her bottom thrust out, and stared up at Frank, all the time rolling her tongue over her lips as though she was still engorging his cock. It was a weird reversal of roles, with Alice acting as sexual factotum to a man who was generally paid to look after her welfare. 'Why don't you fuck me, you wanker,' she hissed at him, and his face crumpled into a condescending smile. His cock was prodding vertically at his belly button, but this man had all the time in the world, and wasn't going to settle for something as simple as a straight fuck. Alice knew she was totally at his disposal, and no immediate moves on his cock would make any impression unless he instigated the action. It was like she was confronting a stranger, and not her uncle's valet, and a stranger possessed of a complex sexual repertoire. Frank, who spent his life obeying orders, was suddenly in direct command of this sexual game.

He commanded Alice to sit on the bed. 'You'll get fucked later,' he said. 'But first I want my pleasure. Take off a stocking and fit it like condom over my cock.' And Alice did so, fitting Frank's cock to the toepiece of her nylon. 'Now place my cock inside your shoe,' and Alice fitted the nyloned head into her pointed stiletto. 'That's it,' moaned Frank. 'Now work me off and finger yourself,' he demanded, and Alice rubbed Frank's cock in and out of her pointed leather shoe as though the latter was her pussy. When he came it was volcanic, and after a pause he was ready to give her what she wanted. Alice kicked her legs up. Her toes were in contact with Elvis Presley. It gave her pleasure to think she was masturbating the King while Frank filled her with the solid cock for which she was aching.

Catching Stars

'Not so fast,' Sandra cautioned, as her lover made to enter her, fitting his body over hers with the sort of intermeshing fluency they had established over months of dynamic sex. 'You haven't heard my story yet, and if you don't interrupt me and just allow yourself to grow excited, then it will be even better.'

Nick rolled over on to his back, his taut erection periscoping for his navel, his willingness to wait being part of the arousal games they had devised to enhance pleasure. It had become a habit. Neither would allow the other orgasmic pleasure until they had exhausted the range of delayed excitation.

'If you don't lie back and listen, I shall have to put you in leather handcuffs again,' Sandra whispered. 'And you'll have to tie my feet in black ribbon to prevent me caressing your penis with my toes. I know how you like that. It takes ages to come, but it's worth it.'

Nick lay back and didn't protest. He knew that Sandra's story would be the prolegomena to some form of perverse sexual geometry. He reached for his champagne glass and listened to the fizz on his tongue. It reminded him of childhood, and how as a boy he had placed a shell to his ear and believed that the roar of his blood was the ocean laying white thunder across the beach. He was wearing a pair of elbow length black silk gloves, for Sandra nurtured an adventurous fetish to have black silk fingers playing over her bottom.

'What I'm going to tell you is completely true,' Sandra added, momentarily slipping under the sheets to place a lipsticked kiss on Nick's cock. 'I was at a private girls' school between the ages of twelve and seventeen. There weren't any boys so we pretended to be them at times. We used to wear bottle green gymslips and pleated games skirts, and little white cotton panties underneath. In order to get out of conventional games like hockey, a number of us gained permission to experiment with juggling. I had silver juggling balls, but other friends used red, pink, green, or blue. It used to look like we were negotiating miniature planets. Sci-fi toys that had somehow dropped out of the sky into our hands. I used to juggle opposite Julie, who defied school convention by wearing black knickers under her games skirt. I used to catch glimpses of them each time she retrieved a dropped ball. I found myself paying scrupulous attention to what all the girls were wearing under their uniforms. We had already elected a place behind the bicycle shed where we taught each other french kissing. I had adopted the role of an imaginary boy called James, and with my hair piled under a beret, the girl I was designated was none other than Julie. Of course this was innocent enough. We began by kissing lightly and then deepening the lips to an oval, and then I advanced my tongue. It went into her mouth like a pink fish and began swimming in her saliva. It felt like I was tasting a new form of fruit, soft and pulpy like melon. When Julie reciprocated the action all the movie kisses we had watched seemed in the process of being consummated. And then suddenly all the girls were doing it. There were eight of us paired off into four couples. It didn't go any further that day, but Julie gave us a wonderful demonstration of three ball juggling, the metallic blue spheres perfectly coordinated in their reach and fall, and Julie occasionally kicking her legs high like a can-can dancer.

Nick leaned over and placed a hot mouth on Sandra's left nipple. He switched to the right with equal effect, and watched her close her eyes in order to luxuriate in the sensation. Then taking out one of the lengths of black ribbon he kept concealed under the pillow, he slid down her body, flickering his tongue over her moist vulva, a crack swollen to the density of a purple pansy, and went all the way down her legs to her ankles.

'You're going to be punished for not telling enough,' Nick warned, and began binding her ankles together with ribbon. He tightened the knot, and confident it was secure, resurfaced for air. 'The next time,' he admonished, 'it will be your thighs and then your wrists. And you'll be begging to be fucked, and unable to get your legs open.'

Sandra moaned at the constriction of her ankles. She arched her legs and importuned 'Lick me. Bury your head between my legs.'

Nick didn't respond. He lay there imperturbable in his sense of cool. 'I want to hear how you licked Julie,' he replied. 'If it wasn't that day, then it was the next one.'

'I'll let you in a little on my secrets,' Sandra volunteered. 'Julie and I began flirting in class. But it was more than the usual schoolgirl thing. It was leading to something serious. Her green eyes would meet mine across the room and I'd catch my breath. And once when we sat next to each other in the French class she placed my hand on her lap. The thrill went through me like lightning. I could feel her warmth and her legs were trembling with excitement. And soon after that there was the occasion when we almost collided in the corridor. Kicked off balance I swung round and our lips became involved in a kiss that went to the roots of my sex. It was then that I knew it would happen. For days I lived in suspense. We seemed to avoid each other in preparation for the meeting when it happened. And meanwhile general activities near the bicycle sheds hadn't diminished. Girls would go there after school to play at being boys. And of course the roles were exchanged. Sometimes we were boys and sometimes girls. Both roles were exciting.'

'You'll have to be punished again, for not telling the

true story,' said Nick, again slipping beneath the sheets and causing Sandra to giggle as he paid attention to her pussy with his tongue. 'Now I'm going to tie your thighs with ribbons,' he remonstrated, and Sandra made playful attempts to elude his designs before submitting to the second phase of her punishment. 'Now I want the real story,' Nick commanded.

'But I shouldn't be telling you these things,' said Sandra. 'You'll begin to think I really like having sex with girls. And perhaps I do. But I'll tell you the story of how Julie and I came together, providing that you release me.'

'Only if it's good enough,' Nick consented. 'If it isn't I'll have to tie your wrists as well.'

'It happened on a Friday morning. I still remember the day exactly. Julie wasn't at lessons that days but her friend Marcella handed me a note. I remember taking it to the toilets and locking myself in a cubicle. And it was there in the conspiratorial quiet that I read Julie's love letter. She told me that she had stayed away from school today as she wanted to lie in bed and think of me. She asked if I would come to her house the next day, on the Saturday evening. She said that her parents were away on holiday in Greece. We would have the place to ourselves.'

'Quicker,' said Nick, 'or you'll have your wrists tied.'

'I spent all afternoon preparing for our rendezvous. I had a long bath, and after the fashion of a Japanese pornographic magazine which had been passed about at school, I depilated myself. I put on a bright red lipstick and a pair of my mother's little black panties which I filched from her drawer. I can remember it all to the last detail. I was so sensitive to touch that I would have jumped if a stranger had even imagined making love to me, I would have seen the idea in his head stand out like a red fish in a transparent bowl.'

'I want more details about your preparation,' said Nick. 'And remember, I may not stop at tying your wrists. There may be further indignities.'

'I wore skintight jeans and a skimpy black jumper, and

a black bra which gave a conical shape to my breasts,' said Sandra. 'I knew precisely what I was entertaining. And when Julie opened the door she looked twenty, and not fifteen. She was dressed in a black leather mini-skirt and sheer seamed tights. She kissed me full on the lips by way of greeting. And that kiss was exploratory, and went so deep into me it was like a probe. Julie poured me a drink. We were neither of us used to alcohol, and the martini cocktail which Julie proportioned placed me somewhere else in my head. The alcohol induced lateral thinking. We were trying to discuss our first readings of Proust, but all the time Julie was sitting opposite me in an armchair with her legs arched, so that I could see right up her skirt. I can't remember at what point she came over and sat on my lap. It was unexpected, but it felt natural. We began kissing, and for the first time my hands wandered to her full breasts. Julie purred, and instructed me to place my hand under her jumper. When I did, she bit my neck from passion, and advised me how to caress her nipples. And I was conscious that she seemed much more sexually experienced than me, but I couldn't work out how she had acquired this knowledge. I think I told myself that she had probably read erotic novels, and knew from those the intimate vocabulary of sensuality. But I was frightened by her excitement. She began to push herself against me, and the breasts which I had extracted from her bra were suddenly being placed in my face. Their nipples were splashed purple. Julie said that the circular zone to each nipple was called the areola. I had areolas. And I was getting stimulated by her excitement. She had placed a hand between her legs while I was arousing her nipples, and now she slipped my hand to that accommodating role.'

'You're going to have to be tied completely,' said Nick, taking out a short length of black ribbon, and proceeding to lick Sandra's breasts as he went in search of her hidden hands. She was sitting on them, and attempted to keep them concealed, so that Nick had to turn her over and spank her round bottom to have her offer her wrists.

'Now I can do what I like with you,' he affirmed. 'I want to hear far more than you're telling me. And stay lying on your stomach, so that I can discipline you if necessary. Without hands or feet there's nothing you can do to retaliate.'

'I was telling you that Julie placed my hand on the wet divide between her legs. She pleaded with me to tickle her. She told me that the man always took the dominant mode of action. And I delighted in tickling her. She slipped out of her tights and skirt with alacrity, so as to give me easier access to her sex. By now I was really getting turned on and losing the inhibitions I may have brought to the game. And what's more, the action I was imparting to her seemed to be transmitted to myself. In tickling her I was tickling myself. That's the good thing about gay sex, you know precisely how the other person feels because you've also been there. There isn't any of that wondering how the opposite receives pleasure involved. And the next thing was that my jeans were being pulled off, and not without effort as they were very tight. Julie said she was going to do something to me that she wished me to copy, and that it would feel incredible. She began kissing my navel and then working her lips lower. I sort of knew what was coming, but couldn't imagine the feeling. Suddenly her lips were hot on my panties, her fingers lifting an elasticated ridge so her tongue could work in underneath. And once I let go and placed my legs over her shoulders the sensation was incredible. I couldn't have imagined it was this good. I found myself relaxed enough to build towards climax, I was shouting for more and more, while she rimmed me with an alacritous tongue.'

'And what did you give her?' Nick commanded, rewarding Sandra for her narrative by running a line of kisses down her spine to the crack of her bottom. He lingered there with his tongue, then worked his way back on the same sensitive route to her nape. She shivered convulsively and bit her lips.

'I gave her the same. She must have performed oral sex

on me for an hour, and then she told me to come upstairs. I went with her to the bedroom, most of my clothes leaving a trail behind me on the living room carpet. And once upstairs she positioned her legs in the way she had positioned mine, and I began to savour her pussy. It was hot and saline and very urgent. I teased it with the tip of my tongue, watching the little bud expand. Julie urged me to put my tongue right in, and later on my fingers. She wanted to feel all of me. Julie began reaching orgasm after orgasm, her clit was so sensitive. We both looked like we had been sitting in a sauna for the evening. We were both so concentrated into pleasure that I didn't hear the bedroom door open.'

'Get on with the story and you'll be properly rewarded,' said Nick. 'But remember, one digression and you'll be additionally bound.'

'I was working away at Julie's clit when I felt a tongue flick across my pussy from behind. I was up on all fours, and the sensation darted like moist fire between my legs. There wasn't any chance to scream, for Julie came forward and sealed my mouth in a long kiss. I couldn't speak, and all the time this tongue was continuing to take liberties with my sex. I was now being held firmly from behind, and Julie hissed in my ear "Don't look round, but it's my brother. I thought I would introduce a real man into the game." My initial feelings of revulsion were disappearing. I could feel his inflamed member brushing against my bottom. It felt like an addition to his body, as though something indomitably hard was struggling to break into me.'

'I suppose it slipped up your crack from the rear, or up your arse?' prompted Nick.

'You forget I was a virgin,' said Sandra. 'It's not that easy to deflower someone. Anyhow, I enjoyed the sensation of being kissed by two people, one from the front and one behind.'

'You're not telling the truth,' warned Nick. 'One more slip and you'll be bound a second time round the thighs.' That said, he went down on her again and tentatively aroused her with his tongue. She pleaded with him to continue, but he came up again for air, and checked that the knots binding her wrists were secure. Under no circumstances would he risk her touching herself at the volcanic core. When he entered her he wanted her to explode.

'I'll tell you more about the game,' Sandra said, 'but carry on licking me.'

Nick refused, despite the fact that his orgasm was tingling as a subtext in his scrotum. 'Tell me the truth,' he demanded.

'I am,' said Sandra. 'I hadn't even turned round to see this brother of Julie's. All I could feel was his tongue and his cock drumming against me. It was huge like yours, and I could feel that it was moist at the tip. Eventually I disengaged myself from their caresses, and fought free of the boy's urgency. He was made up to look like a girl, something that evidently excited him. His lips were a smudged strawberry lipstick, and the inexpert application of eyeliner had him appear as though he had two black eyes. His face was white with foundation. Julie informed me that he wanted me to put on my dark green games skirt and white cotton panties, and blow him.

'I went even further. I dressed in Julie's mother's stockings and suspenders and sat in front of him nibbling an apple with my legs wide open. We decided to take it in turn. Julie began by licking her brother's cock, and I was the support act. You know it's not uncommon for brothers and sisters at that age to play with each other. It's only a game. He began to grow visibly more excited, and I took over. At that age I'd never sucked cock. I was surprised how big it was in my mouth. And in order to make him wait I'd leave off for a few seconds, take a bite from my red apple, and resume sucking in a disinterested manner. We were so precocious, and he loved it. Julie left me to it, and went and sat on the sofa and tickled herself in her black knickers to add to her brother's excitement. He was moaning now, and the whole length of his cock began to twitch. I could hardly contain his thrusts, and then his come began to decant in hot spurts. It went on and on. It was like catching stars. White-hot shooting stars in my mouth. Star after star after star. And if he fucked me later, I'm not going to tell until you do.'

'I have to untie some of the ribbons first,' said Nick, and he began with the ankles and the thighs and then the waist. He would leave her hands tied. And when he entered her it was with explosive urgency. And she, as his urgency increased, tickled his balls with a single finger, the one on which she wore a ring decorated with stars.

After Wilde's Trial

Jeanette sat reading a yellow backed French novel. It was Pierre Louys's forbidden *Aphrodite*, a book found offensive by the authorities. She was dressed in a long black satin dress, with black petticoats underneath, and her ankles showed a glimpse of silk stocking between the hem and her shoes. She was waiting for her lover in the red drawing room, the lamp lit, and heavy rain falling outside.

    Jeanette was impatient, aroused, but delighted in the period of suspense before her servant would enter the room and announce William's arrival. They were opposites. Jeanette devoted her time to the arts, while William was a banker in the city. A part of her despised him, and the games she played with him brought out her sadism at the expense of his naivety. She continued to read, and let her right hand stray under her heavy skirt. But she wouldn't allow herself the appeasing motion of her finger on her pussy. She delayed, aware of how she was wearing split black silk panties under her petticoats. She had them hand-made for her in Paris, according to the style used by can-can dancers to excite the audience. She let her hand rest on her thigh at the level of her garter, and pretended it was a stranger's crept there illicitly during a theatre performance. Jeanette fantasised about such things, a man's hand exploring her crotch anonymously. When they got up from their seats, each would take a different direction to the exit. Jeanette liked to employ this trick when she was in public libraries or out riding in a cab. It was a sort of reassuring risk.

She had even done it to herself in William's company, and he being unobservant had gone on reading, oblivious to the tantalising rustle of her skirts.

Jeanette's mind was straying from the novel. She took a small glass of green absinthe and let it tincture her lips. Ever since the scandalous court case involving Oscar Wilde, she had developed a fascination for his habits. Absinthe was one of them, green carnations another. William was shocked by her decadent traits, and had given up taking her to parties, claiming that she would embarrass him in polite company. And far from being offended Jeanette had waited her time, inviting him regularly to her house, and secretly planning a form of vengeance. She had all the time in the world to read up on back issues of Wilde's trial, and to form plans to avenge herself on her conventional fiancé.

She heard the clock strike seven. Wilde she read had been considered a moral danger to the young, a corrupting influence on male youth. He was considered the velvet coated toff who buggered rough trade, particularly in the beds of the Ritz and the Savoy. William wouldn't have the man's name mentioned. He would put his paper in front of his face and say, 'Don't you dare mention that name in front of me. The man should be struck off all social registers.' Jeanette inwardly laughed at these absurd displays of prejudice coming from a city banker who was so reluctant to own to a cock in her company. He promised that after marriage he would thrash her in the sheets. Still, she would give him one more chance.

At seven fifteen her servant discreetly knocked and entered. He announced William, who was making a big fuss about the London rain and how the cabbie had not sufficiently sheltered him with an umbrella on his stepping out of the cab to reach the front door. The man should have received a sound whipping, he was saying, for this indiscretion. Anyhow he would trace his employer and see to it that he was dismissed.

William settled to his usual scotch and water, while Jeanette who had hardly looked up from her book, continued reading. She held the yellow cover face out, but the book's notoriety seemed unknown to a man who had once impressed her by his quiet melancholy. He had told her initially of his love of poetry, but his taste in the latter had proved to be the sleepiest areas of Tennyson's late verse.

Jeanette let him settle, then kicked off one satin slipper, wriggled her stockinged toes in the air, and then repeated the gesture. She had bought the sheerest silk stockings, and had painted her toenails red, a touch that she had derived not only from reading French novels, but from visiting brothels in the East End. There she had paid to be concealed, to look through peep-holes and two way mirrors. She had observed extraordinary things, and these in turn had her long to develop her sexual expertise. She had seen a couple in the 69 position, the women up on her haunches facing the opposite direction to the man, her pussy lowered to his mouth, while hers fitted over his erection. She had seen men being corrected by birches, and women dressed in scarlet waspies whipping fat bureaucrats over nursery chairs, Her excitement at these times could hardly be contained. And better still she had watched a woman strip slowly, item by item, the man unallowed to touch her until half an hour later she was completely naked. It was this game she intended to play with William.

She had her feet caress each other, the slight friction of the silk creating a provocation which should instate instant curiosity and arousal. But there was no response. William was talking to her about his day at the office, and the report he had prepared on shares in the declining company of Elder and Jones, city merchants. Fired by his first scotch he was feeling additionally sure of his merits. 'I've burnt their boats,' he was saying, 'miserable bastards will go right under now. People think they can go on borrowing a lifetime. We're not prepared to have it. You'd have been proud of me. The way I handled them was a storm.'

Unable to attract attention with her stocking toes, Jeanette manoeuvred her hem up past her ankles, that part of a woman's body which had provoked most outrage amongst moralists and which had correspondingly developed into a fetish amongst those who spent their time observing women getting into or out of carriages, or lifting their skirts to climb carpeted stairs to the ballroom.

Jeanette had chosen black silk petticoats with red lace borders. They reminded her of the ones worn by girls in the better houses down by the river, where men arrived in hansoms in the fog, and under cover of disguise entered establishments where red lights burnt all day and night. Surely, she thought, the naughtiness of this underwear would have William break his reserve. But he continued to speak as though nothing was happening. He was still certain that his petty office affairs were of universal importance, and would have him shine in her eyes. He was well into his second large scotch, and he toyed with the tumbler as though it emphasised the strength of his manly actions. But as Jeanette increased the amount of slip showing, so that her petticoats began to lift above her calves, so William fixed his eyes on the painting just to the left of her, a point of focus that he had come to develop as his own in his reluctance to make eye contact. At first she had taken this for an endearingly shy characteristic, but the habit had turned boring, and usually implied that he was about to deliver an unwelcome monologue.

'Fuck it,' she thought secretly. 'I'll end up frigging myself off in front of him, fingers pushed through my crotchless panties. And even then he'll just keep on talking.' But instead, she crossed her long curved legs, and lifted her skirt up above her knees. The prospect of what he was seeing made her excited. She was imagining herself as a man would. She knew that if she was him, an erection would be straining at the fly. She would nuzzle a head under her skirts and begin, and soon have her legs up there on the couch. But he showed no interest, and continued speaking to the picture on the wall.

She decided to go further, and hitched her skirt up to her thighs, so that the red garter worn at the top was almost visible, and would be in the next stage of her provocation. She placed the yellow book in her lap as a decadent gesture. She was hoping he would come over, take up the title and have the message click. Rain kept streaming against the glass, she could hear its assault on the other side of the curtain. It was the perfect time for him to pick her up behind her legs, and carry her upstairs in a black froth of lingerie. She could hardly bear it. She had now inched the skirt up above her frilly garter, and suspected that bracelet of lace would prove irresistible. She was moist and ready for his advance. She would have shrieked with desire if he had come over and ravished her. But he didn't, he kept on with his absurd list of achievements, extending it to how he had got his valet reading Trollope in between his various duties.

Unable to seduce her man, Jeanette gave him a momentary glance of her slit silk panties, and noticing a flicker of repressed interest, decided to put her plan into action. She had the day before recruited the services of a twenty year old gigolo, a handsome stud who could fuck for hours on end without getting tired. She had him upstairs waiting for her. He was lying in the sheets of her four poster, and wearing a pair of her silk French knickers.

'I'm going upstairs to dress for dinner, William,' she said without the least sense of frustration entering her voice. 'It will take me twenty minutes to prepare, and I want you to knock on my door after twenty minutes. My maid is away on leave, and I will have to ask you to deal with a number of little fastenings. Nothing complicated or likely to embarrass. You're probably not interested in French novels, but you can read mine if you like, while I'm upstairs preparing. I promise you there's nothing about Wilde in the text.'

Jeanette bustled slinkily out of the drawing room. All those black silks sitting on her skin had her feel like one of the girls working in the mirrored bedroom of a brothel. She knew that in time, just to experience the bizarre fetishes demanded by a range of clients, she would admit herself to such an establishment, and work there in secrecy. 'And be exact about the twenty minutes, William,' she called out before climbing the stairs.

When she opened the bedroom door, he was waiting in bed. She could see his erection poking up like a tent pole in the sheets. The anticipation had aroused him to impatience. This young man called James was not without refinement. Although he came from the countryside, and had experienced no formal education, and had finally run away to find adventure in the city, he read books, and appreciated them for the aesthetic content. She had come across him in Kensington Gardens. He was sitting on a bench reading a little green and gold book of poetry. She had discovered that it was *Silverpoints*, the first collection by an up and coming young poet called John Gray. The young man professed to know the poet, and to occasionally socialise with his circle. And Jeanette had found herself attracted by this blend of country looks and city taste. She had taken him back home in her carriage, and wanting the matter to remain secret she had paid him to conduct their affair in secrecy. And being bribed appealed to him. He had made money like this before. Society women had paid for his body. He saw nothing dishonourable in it. He gave and received pleasure. That he could have caused major scandals by his knowledge was something he either cared not to discuss or was in the process of silently waiting for an opportune occasion. Jeanette didn't care. He could gossip about her as he wished. All that concerned her was to be engorged by his ten inch cock, a weapon that was near perfect in its circumcised proportions, and its ability to have her feel as though her legs were spread across the room. And his knowledge of sex was extraordinary for such a young man. Unlike the other youths who she had paid to have, and who, faced by her long legs and full breasts had shown an urgency that had left her unsatisfied, James was a master of control, his modulated thrusts bringing her off again and again in a series of ecstatic orgasms. And he knew well how to excite her with his tongue, burying it in her like it was a second and differently expressive cock.

She sat down on the bed, while his trembling fingers began to undo the hook and eye fastenings that kept up her satin dress. She was in a bra popping red and black waspie underneath, and the dress undone, she went over to the mirror, and took off layer after layer of black silk, and then stood there in nothing but her waspie, slit panties and silk stockings with the red frilly garter. She pushed her bottom out towards him, for he delighted in its round proportions. One glimpse of it, he would say, and he was insatiably horny.

She stood there unpinning her hair, and letting the luxurious red ringlets scatter over her shoulders. 'I want you to do something for me, James, it's an unusual request. My fiancé is downstairs, or rather the man who was my fiancé, for his inconsideration and dullness know no limits. I've decided to punish him, and I don't want to see him ever again. I've told him to come upstairs and help me with my dress in twenty minutes, or what is fifteen now. I want you to put on this wig, darling, and pretend you're me. Your reward for this will be to have the right to go up my back passage tonight, as well as my front. I want you to wear my scantiest underwear, and to look irresistible. Pull him on to the bed, entangle him in your stockinged legs, and let him discover to his horror that you're a man. Please do this for me. You will be well rewarded in every way. But we must hurry.'

James was only too willing to take part in the experiment. Jeanette dressed him in a sumptuous red wig, a black satin basque, and a pair of silk French knickers that did little to hide his bulging crotch. She applied a red lipstick to his pouting lips, and dusted his face with white powder. She turned the lamps down, and had the bedroom lit by a single candle, the better to disguise James's figure. But she felt herself aroused by the sight of him in drag. He had the body with which to flaunt her lingerie. She was disquieted that he warmed to it so easily, treating it not as a game, but as something that seemed like second nature. The thought came to her that he had done this before. He was accomplished in things in which she was clumsy. He took over from her directions, and applied his own makeup, rucked out the red wig, and without asking her, took emerald earrings from her jewel box, and knew without consulting the mirror that he was wearing them with style. Jeanette felt shocked at his transformation. She wanted to lift his heavy cock out of the black silk to reassure herself that she could still make it rise. She tickled him lightly and felt the immediate response, but there wasn't much time. William would come upstairs soon, and the deception would begin. She liked to think of him rushing out of the room in a state of shock, open mouthed, unable to speak, and going out into the heavy night rain to get saturated while he waited for a cab. He would curse her to the ends of the world, while she lay warm inside, James's massive dick pumping her from one side of the bed to the other. Her servant, excited by the noise of her shrieks would stand outside the keyhole, his hand buried in his fly.

They lay together on the bed, Jeanette's lips circling the head of James's enraged member. She sipped at it, all the time listening out for William's footsteps on the broad wooden stairs. And sure enough they heard him. He came slowly down the length of the passage, stopped outside her bedroom door and hesitantly knocked. Jeanette got up from the bed and slipped into her adjoining dressing room, leaving the door faintly ajar so that she could witness the turn of events.

James went over to the door with absolute assurance, fluffing up his hair in the process. Jeanette felt instantly jealous that he should upstage her feminine qualities. He even had a natural wiggle as he balanced on her heels.

She held her breath and watched as he slowly unlocked the door, and opened it by slow degrees. He placed one motioning finger through the divide, then two, then three. It was a lesson in the art of seduction. When he opened the door wider it was to extend his tongue, and to Jeanette's horror she saw that it was being received on the other side. James was passionately kissing her fiancé. She couldn't call out, so she watched as the sequence of events unclosed. The door was now open and his arms were around William's shoulders, walking him backwards towards the bed as he kissed him. Jeanette saw her frigid boyfriend responding with reciprocal passion as the two of them collapsed onto the bed. James was acting as a real woman, fondling William between the thighs, taking him again and again into more prolonged kisses, placing his hands on his stockinged thighs. Jeanette kept telling herself that of course it was an act, and that within a very short time William would be out in the street, white faced, traumatised, and James's big cock would be impaling her with its angry thrusts. She was beginning to feel a real love for her country boy, and wanted to keep him in her house, for fear he would find pleasure elsewhere.

    She looked on in pain as the two caressed each other, and when they rolled over so that James was on top of William, she knew it was impossible that the latter wouldn't feel James's erection. She consoled herself with the thought that he was probably slack, as there was no chance that William's unengaging body would arouse him. Or was he really imagining that William was her, had he forgotten that this was an act, and that it would be he, rather than William who recoiled with distaste. But they were going too far. William who had ignored her every layer of black froth, now had his hands inserted down the back of James's silk knickers. He was forcing them down and extending his hand to cup James's balls. At the same time James was tearing off William's clothes, and Jeanette reeled backwards as she saw William's erection enter her lover's mouth. She closed the door to her dressing room, and stood there wide eyed looking into the mirror as she heard the telltale sounds of the bed rhythmically creaking.

velvet

THE LUSTS OF THE LIBERTINES
The Marquis De Sade

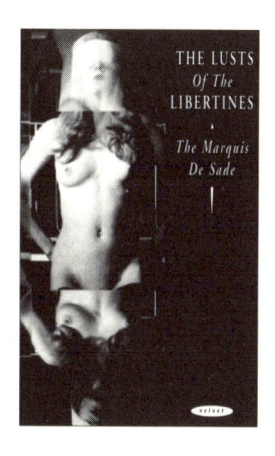

The Circle of Manias, the Circle of Excrement, the Circle of Blood; three gateways to a living Hell envisaged by the Marquis de Sade as he simmered in the bowels of the Bastille. An infernal zone where Libertines are free to pursue and execute their every caprice, no matter how depraved or inhuman.

Here, in a brand new, unexpurgated and explicit translation, are the 447 "complex, criminal and murderous lusts" of the Libertines as documented by de Sade in his accursed atrocity bible *The 120 Days Of Sodom;* a catalogue of debaucheries, cruelties and pathological perversions still unequalled in the annals of transgressive literature.

DUNGEON EVIDENCE: *Correct Sadist II*
Terence Sellers

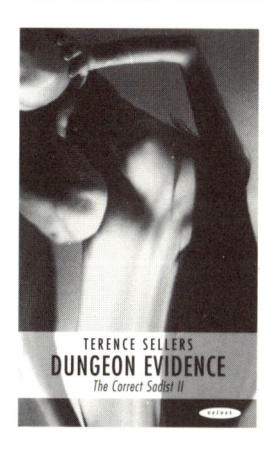

The Mistress Angel Stern presides without mercy over a New York dungeon where her slaves, the "morally insane" of modern society, obey her every whim and undergo any degradation she wills upon them.

In the closed confines of a torture zone, these paraphiliacs and sexual malcontents use her image as an object for their masturbatory depravities, craving her cruelty in an abyss of sadomasochism and bondage.

Here are the bizarre case histories, philosophies and psychopathologies of a dominatrix; a frank testament which reveals not only the drives which lead some to become slaves, but also the complex exchange of psychic energies involved in scenes of dominance and submission.

THE VELVET UNDERGROUND
Michael Leigh

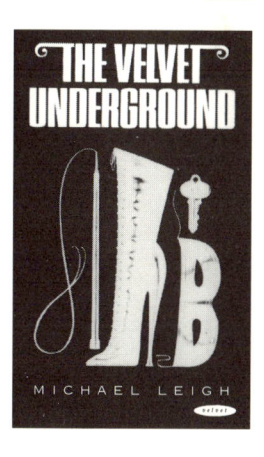

Swingers and swappers, strippers and streetwalkers, sadists, masochists, and sexual mavericks of every persuasion; all are documented in this legendary exposé of the diseased underbelly of '60s American society.

The Velvet Underground is the ground-breaking sexological study that lent its name to the seminal New York rock'n'roll group, whose songs were to mirror its themes of depravity and social malaise.

Welcome to the sexual twilight zone, where the death orgies of Altamont and Helter Skelter are just a bull-whip's kiss away.

VELVET PUBLICATIONS

velvet

SISTER MIDNIGHT *Jeremy Reed*

The Marquis de Sade is dead – but his sister is alive and well, stalking the ruins of the château of La Coste where she reconstructs the apocalyptic orgies, tortures and blasphemies of her brother's reviled last will and testament, *The 120 Days Of Sodom*.

Castle freaks, killing gardens, lesbian love trysts on human furniture; these and countless other configurations of debauched carnality conspire and collude in a sundered, dream-like zone where the clock strikes eternal midnight.

Sister Midnight is the sequel to Jeremy Reed's erotic classic *The Pleasure Château*, a continued exploration of decadent extremes and sexual delirium in the tradition of de Sade, Sacher-Masoch and Apollinaire; a tribute to undying lust and the endless scope of human perversion.

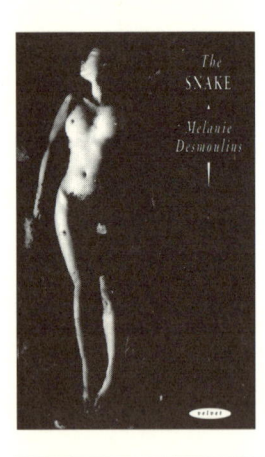

THE SNAKE *Melanie Desmoulins*

When Lucy, a sexually frustrated young widow, is mysteriously sent a plane ticket to Portugal, she takes a flight into erotic abandon which can only lead to death and damnation.

Soon seduced by both a debauched Englishwoman and her Portuguese husband, she sheds the skin of morality like a snake and begins to act out her darkest, uninhibited sexual desires. Increasingly depraved rituals of narcotics abuse, Satanism and sadomasochism – presided over by Bartolomeo, a Sade-like albino cult leader – eventually lead to the total disintegration of Lucy's ego.

At Bartolomeo's isolated villa, a shrine to pornographic art and literature, she finally enters the snake pit...

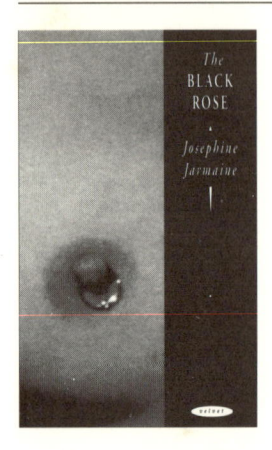

THE BLACK ROSE *Josephine Jarmaine*

Abducted to a mysterious French island, sixteen-year-old Rosamund finds herself at the mercy of the Duke and his four libidinous sons. She soon learns that her virginity must be sacrificed in order to breed the Black Rose, a rare flower whose aphrodisiac elixir will transform the world into a polysexual playground of orgiastic and orgasmic excess.

Rosamund's carnal initiation plunges her into a vortex of pain and pleasure, as she discovers that the Château Rose is a sensory realm where sadism, sapphism, sodomy, incest, bestiality, bondage and rampant fornication are a way of life.

The Black Rose is a stunning hybrid of decadence and explicit sexuality, a unique modern classic.

VELVET PUBLICATIONS

velvet

PHILOSOPHY IN THE BOUDOIR *The Marquis de Sade*

In the boudoir of a sequestered country house, a young virgin is ruthlessly schooled in evil. Indoctrinated by her amoral tutors in the ways of sexual perversion, fornication, murder, incest, atheism and complete self-gratification, she takes part with growing abandon in a series of violent erotic orgies which culminates with the flagellation and torture of her own mother – her final act of liberation.

Philosophy In The Boudoir is the most concise, representative text out of all the Marquis de Sade's works, containing his notorious doctrine of libertinage expounded in full, coupled with liberal doses of savage, unbridled eroticism, cruelty and violent sexuality. The renegade philosophies put forward here would later rank amongst the main cornerstones of André Breton's Surrealist manifesto.

THE SHE-DEVILS *Pierre Louÿs*

A mother and her three daughters...sharing their inexhaustible sexual favours between the same young man, each other, and anyone else who enters their web of depravity. From a chance encounter on the stairway with a voluptuous young girl, the narrator is drawn to become the plaything of four rapacious females, experiencing them all in various combinations of increasingly wild debauchery, until they one day vanish as mysteriously as they had appeared.

Described by Susan Sontag as one of the few works of the erotic imagination to deserve true literary status, *The She Devils (Trois Filles De Leur Mère)* remains Pierre Louÿs' most intense, claustrophobic work; a study of sexual obsession and mono-mania unsurpassed in its depictions of carnal excess, unbridled lust and limitless perversity.

THE PLEASURE CHATEAU *Jeremy Reed*

The story of Leanda, mistress of an opulent château, who tirelessly indulges her compulsion for sexual extremes, entertaining deviants, transsexuals and freaks in pursuit of the ultimate erotic experience. She is finally transported to a zone where sex transcends death, and existence becomes a never-ending orgy of the senses. The book also includes *Tales Of The Midget*, astonishing erotic adventures as related by a dwarf raconteur versed in decades of debauch.

Jeremy Reed, hailed as one of the greatest poets of his generation, has turned his exquisite imagination to producing this masterpiece of gothic erotica in the tradition of de Sade, Apollinaire and Sacher-Masoch, his tribute to the undying flame of human sexuality.

FLESH UNLIMITED *Guillaume Apollinaire*

The debauched aristocrat Mony Vibescu and a circle of fellow sybarites blaze a trail of uncontrollable lust, cruelty and depravity across the streets of Europe. A young man reminisces his sexual awakening at the hands of his aunt, his sister and their friends as he is irremediably corrupted in a season of carnal excess.

Flesh Unlimited is a compendium edition of *Les Onze Mille Verges* and *Les Mémoires d'Un Jeune Don Juan*, Apollinaire's two wild masterpieces of the explicit erotic imagination, works which compare with the best of the Marquis de Sade.

Presented in brand new translations by Alexis Lykiard (translator of Lautréamont's *Maldoror*), these are the original, complete and unexpurgated versions, with full introduction and notes.

VELVET PUBLICATIONS

velvet

INFORMATION

You have just read a *Velvet* book
Published by:
Velvet Publications
83, Clerkenwell Road, London EC1R 5AR
Tel: 0171-430-9878 Fax: 0171-242-5527
E-mail: velvet@pussycat.demon.co.uk

Velvet publications should be available in all proper bookstores; please ask your local retailer to order from:

UK & Europe: Turnaround Distribution, Unit 3 Olympia Trading Estate, Coburg Road, Wood Green, London N22 6TZ
Tel: 0181-829-3000 Fax: 0181-881-5088

Italy: Apeiron Editoria & Distribuzione
Pizza Orazio Moroni 4
00060 Sant'Oresta (Roma)
Tel: 0761-579670
Fax: 0761-579737

USA: Subterranean Company, Box 160, 265 South 5th Street, Monroe, OR 97456
Tel: 541-847-5274 Fax: 541-847-6018

USA Non-booktrade: Xclusiv, 451 50th St, Brooklyn, NY 11220
Tel: 718-439-1271 Fax: 718-439-1272
Last Gasp, 777 Florida St, San Francisco, CA 94110
Tel: 415-824-6636 Fax: 415-824-1836
AK Distribution, PO Box 40682, San Francisco, CA 94140-0682
Tel: 415-864-0892 Fax: 415-864-0893

Canada: Marginal, Unit 102, 277 George Street, N. Peterborough, Ontario K9J 3G9
Tel/Fax: 705-745-2326

Japan: Tuttle-Shokai, 21-13 Seki 1-Chome, Tama-ku, Kawasaki, Kanagawa 214
Tel: 44-833-1924 Fax: 44-833-7559

A full catalogue is available on request.

ORDER FORM

(please photocopy if you do not wish to cut up your book)

TITLE *(please tick box)*	PRICE	QUANTITY	TITLE *(please tick box)*	PRICE	QUANTITY
☐ The Lusts Of The Libertines	£7.95		☐ Flesh Unlimited	£7.95	
☐ Dungeon Evidence	£9.95		☐ The Whip Angels	£4.95	
☐ The Velvet Underground	£7.95		☐ House Of Pain	£4.95	
☐ Whiplash Castle	£7.95		☐ Irene's Cunt	£7.95	
☐ The Snake	£7.95		☐ Psychopathia Sexualis	£9.95	
☐ The Black Rose	£7.95		☐ Torture Garden	£16.95	
☐ Philosophy In The Boudoir	£7.95		☐ Baby Doll	£12.95	
☐ The She Devils	£7.95		☐ City Of The Broken Dolls	£12.95	
☐ The Pleasure Château	£7.95		☐ Heat	£14.95	

Total Amount £_____ ☐ I enclose cheque/money order   ☐ I wish to pay by ☐ Visa ☐ Mastercard

Card No: |___|___|___|___|___|___|___|___|___|___|___|___|___|___|___|___| Expiry_____

Signature_____Date_____

Name_____

Address_____

_____Telephone_____

Please add 10% to total price for postage & packing in UK (max. £5.00) 20% outside UK (max £10.00).
Make cheques/money orders payable to **Velvet Publications** and send to 83 Clerkenwell Road, London EC1R 5AR (Sterling only)

VELVET PUBLICATIONS